A SOUND IN THE DARK

KYLE ALEXANDER ROMINES

ALSO BY KYLE ALEXANDER ROMINES

The Keeper of the Crows (Sunbury Press)
The Chrononaut

This book is dedicated to anyone who has ever wanted to give up.

"Do not set foot in the path of the wicked or walk in the way of evildoers. Avoid it, do not travel on it; turn from it and go on your way. For they cannot rest until they do evil; they are robbed of sleep till they make someone stumble. They eat the bread of wickedness and drink the wine of violence."

—Proverbs 4:14-19

PROLOGUE

THE SUN ROSE SLOWLY OVER the horrors below, which were left behind like a child's misplaced toy. Despite the early hour, the park was already unbearably hot. The formidable temperature was typical of the Texas climate, usually offset by the region's great beauty. Today that beauty was marred. The Elmore State Park would ordinarily be teeming with camping enthusiasts, heat notwithstanding. This was not an ordinary day. The only people in the park at the moment were park staff and law enforcement officers.

A car pulled into a makeshift parking area just outside a barrier of yellow tape. The car's driver was a man named Frank Collins, an unassuming detective who would've otherwise been doing little aside from mulling retirement. Frank knew little about the scene that was waiting for him other than it was a multiple homicide investigation and currently the department's number one priority.

The detective stepped out of the car and immediately found himself face-to-face with two troopers. Although Frank didn't know the two men from Adam, they seemed familiar with him.

"Detective Frank," one of the troopers said almost immediately.

"That's me," he answered curtly.

The two troopers glanced briefly at each other before the first man spoke again.

"Why don't you follow us this way?"

Frank followed along quietly. Neither trooper said anything else right away, though they occasionally exchanged nervous glances. If these two men were supposed to brief him, it wasn't off to a particularly promising start.

"I'm Jim Stillwell, by the way," the first man said after a time. "And this is Ramon Burgess."

The troopers led Frank down a dirt trail that ran through the park. A short time later, they emerged in a clearing inaccessible by vehicles. A tent rested just outside the bushes. There was already a group of officers surrounding the area.

Frank sensed something was wrong even before he saw the blood. A dark red patch streaked down one side of the duly colored tent, which was twisted, as if improperly set up.

"What happened here?" Frank whispered almost too softly for the others to hear. As he neared the tent, several of the officers broke into groups to begin their respective tasks.

Stillwell caught Frank's expression. "You haven't seen anything yet."

Frank wasn't sure what he meant by that. Before Stillwell could elaborate, Frank noticed an elderly man hunched over an out-of-place chair. The man was speaking to three officers. A cup of coffee sat ignored in his hand.

"Who's that?" Frank asked.

"Gerald Mosby, the Park Ranger. He found the first body during his patrol this morning."

Mosby was talking, but the man's eyes remained unfocused. He was clearly in shock.

"How many victims are there?" Frank finally asked.

"We still don't know at this point," Stillwell said. The officer nodded in the direction of a comely brunette now talking to Mosby. "Jeannette found the bodies in the tent."

Frank noted the use of the plural. Officer Ramon finally spoke up, interrupting the detective's thoughts.

"Another two bodies have been discovered since we arrived. There's one in the woods and another at the bottom of a cliff less than a mile away."

"We've got teams spreading out all over the valley," Stillwell finished.

Frank recalled the number of vehicles in the parking lot and nodded. He was starting to feel like he was the wrong man for the job. He was a seasoned officer only recently transferred to a new city, but he'd never encountered anything remotely like this before. How was something like this even feasible?

"You might want to call in more teams," he said uneasily, as if someone hadn't thought of that already.

The killings brought to mind a set of violent murders in another national park a little over a year ago. The murderer had never been found. The press had dubbed the killer 'The Hunter.' Could this be the work of the same individual? Frank didn't even want to think about that possibility.

"I heard the FBI has already been notified," Stillwell said.

A bullhorn sounded in the distance. Frank heard shouts coming from the woods. He knew what that meant. The men turned back the way they came until they reached a spot near the parking lot where terrain vehicles were waiting for them. They followed several other officers, driving deep into the heart of the forest where the air was thick.

Dozens of officers had already assembled. As he stepped out of the vehicle, Frank searched for the source of the commotion. When he turned his head, the officer vomited.

Suspended by ropes, hanging upside-down from a tree, was a mutilated body.

CHAPTER ONE

Z ACK FOUND HIMSELF UNABLE TO speak. His entire body trembled with rage. He slammed shaking hands down loudly against the kitchen countertop. The hands whitened against the black marble surface. She started toward him, and he found his voice. When he spoke, his eyes burned with anger.

"Get out," he said.

That was then. The memory from the past kept repeating itself, like a broken record tearing its way through his skull. The event unfolded over a year ago, but Zack still couldn't rid himself of the scene in the kitchen. Time didn't work. Neither did counseling. Deep down, he wasn't even sure he wanted to be free.

"Watch out!" a voice shouted.

An old pickup truck pulled in front of him, and Zack's foray into the past was cut short. Zack barely had any time to react. He swerved into the right lane, a dangerous gamble considering the van's current speed. He missed the truck by seconds. Zack heard a loud honk, evidence of the displeasure of another driver in the right lane. Having nearly caused a wreck, he couldn't blame the driver for being angry with him.

"Well, that's a great way to start the trip," Dave said lightly after a few seconds.

No one laughed. Dave sighed and shifted against the back seat. Zack caught a glimpse of him in the rearview mirror. There was clear disappointment on his face. Although most of the passengers in the van were Zack's friends, he couldn't say the same about Dave. It was easy to see that Dave was expecting a more jovial environment. Instead, there was an undercurrent of tension since the group started on the road. Zack was aware he was at least partially responsible for that.

He looked over at Will, who sat in the passenger seat next to him. There was caution in his eyes, mingled with another emotion Zack couldn't discern. His friend knew better than to say anything about their near miss. Will's insistence was the only reason Zack was even in the van in the first place.

"You're working too hard," Will had said. "It's time for you to get out of the house for a change."

This sounded all well and good over drinks, but Will didn't exactly share his workload. Zack worked around the clock managing his own bakery, whereas Will was a fulltime partier and womanizer currently studying law (if Will's assertion that taking a few online criminal justice courses constituted studying law was correct).

Camping wasn't completely out of the ordinary for either of them. In fact, they'd gone on such trips regularly in the past. Zack met Will Bradley when the two shared a dorm room his freshman year of college. In what seemed in Zack's experience a rare student housing success, the two became fast friends. Both shared a love of the outdoors, which led to large outings with friends.

Since then, Zack hadn't gone camping in years. His responsibilities at the bakery were part of the reason why. As for the other part...his zeal for life wasn't what it once was, to say the least.

"It's too early in the morning for yelling," Cole Wallace said in a partial growl from the back. Sitting to Dave's left, Cole had propped a massive pillow against the mirror to block out the light and was fighting a losing battle to remain asleep.

Zack smiled. *Leave it to Cole to defuse a tense situation,* he thought. Never mind that they'd almost been killed.

Cole closed his eyes and thrust his head against the pillow. His curly brown hair was completely disheveled. His face didn't look quite the same without the reading glasses Zack had grown accustomed to seeing. Cole must've abandoned them for the trip in favor of contacts.

Like Will, Cole purported to be a law student. Unlike Will, he actually took it seriously. Quiet and thoughtful by nature, Cole was perhaps the most scholarly individual Zack had ever met. Zack suspected it had taken just as much cajoling on Will's part to get Cole to go as it did for himself.

"Why is he even trying to sleep?" Will asked, amused. "We can't be much farther from the park."

"I heard that," Cole replied motionlessly. He yawned, which prompted Zack to do the same. Zack was normally a morning person, but he hadn't slept well for a long time now. He wasn't looking forward to the prospect of a couple of nights on the cold, hard ground.

"Actually, we're less than ten minutes away," Zack said. "You should start waking up."

"I will when we get there," Cole promised.

"You've had hours to sleep," Will insisted.

"You would've had more if Will hadn't insisted on roughing it completely," Zack muttered. He looked at the map. "'No GPS,' you said. 'We'll find it the old fashioned way.'"

Will shook his head. "We're not going to let these two losers ruin the fun for the rest of us, are we guys?"

"What fun?" Dave asked. "It's too early for drinking, and this van is about as lively as a cemetery."

Zack was tempted to ask if Dave wanted to take his chances on the road, but kept his mouth shut.

"You'll see," Will had said when he proposed the trip. "A weekend away is just what you need."

Although Zack admired Will's optimism, he wondered if his friend was ever going to see things as they actually were. He was twenty-eight now. The life they'd known in college would have to end soon for him. It ended long ago for Zack. Still, Zack wasn't in any position to give life advice, so again he remained silent.

"I'm with you, man," said Steve, the person on Dave's right. "I've been waiting for a chance to get away forever."

"That's more like it," Will said.

Steve Emerson was the fifth and final member of their group. Zack knew Steve better than he knew Dave, though even that wasn't saying much. Steve was more Will's friend than anyone's. To Zack's recollection, the two worked a job together one summer.

Altogether, it was a relatively small group by Will's standards. In the old days they'd often required multiple vehicles to carry all the people and supplies. Years passed and friends got married or found employment in other states, causing the circle's numbers to dwindle.

Zack glanced out the window. A sign confirmed that the park entrance was a mere ten miles away. "We're almost there."

The scenery beyond the road certainly seemed promising. Maybe he would enjoy himself after all.

"In one piece, too," Dave said with a smirk, a not-so subtle reference to their near-wreck a few miles back.

Zack felt his temper rise. He wasn't going to put up with Dave's attitude for long.

"This is it," Will said. "Drifter's Folly Memorial Park."

"What part about sleep don't you guys understand?" Cole demanded. He sat up, one hand on the pillow.

"Will was just telling us about the park," Steve said.

"Here we go again," Cole said. "Why don't you tell us all one *more* time how you found the great location of the trip?"

Zack joined in. "While you do, you might mention how big the park is and how it's virtually empty for this time of year."

"Everyone's a critic," Will replied with a grin. "Once you all see what this place has to offer, you'll change your minds."

"As long as we don't get mauled to death first," Dave said.

At that, Will stopped smiling. "It took me a lot of effort to plan this trip. I would appreciate a little gratitude."

"Sorry," Dave said. "It's just cramped in here, that's all."

With that, the temporary enmity was forgotten. Moodiness was one of Will's biggest character flaws, though Zack thought Dave deserved the rebuke. He slid the map onto the dashboard and pulled off the highway.

"At least the weather shouldn't give us any problems," Cole said sleepily. He was checking the forecast on his cell phone.

"It's mid-September," Will replied. "It'll be nice and cool."

Zack remembered a time when they tried camping in November at a lake about an hour from the university. Will dared Cole to go swimming in the lake at night. The water was near freezing, and Cole was so cold he hadn't slept properly the rest of the night. Cole was gone when everyone woke up, having sought refuge for warmth in his car and driven home hours earlier. Zack shook his head at the pleasant memory. What happened to those days?

"Drifter's Folly," he mused. "That's an unusual name. Any reason for it?"

Will shrugged. "Not that I'm aware of. Maybe we'll find out."

Zack nodded. "Maybe."

"Look at the size of those mountains," Steve said, obviously excited. "We can get some good hiking in there."

"I didn't know you were into hiking," Cole said in approval. "Colorado is a perfect place for it."

Zack knew Cole had seen bigger mountains in the past, but he didn't want to ruin the moment for Steve. It was Steve's first camping trip with the group. Dave had gone before, just never with Zack.

Steve and Cole seemed to be getting along well, which was good. In a way the two were quite similar. Both men were loners by nature. Steve wasn't particularly scholarly, though, and often came across as out of place.

"I'm looking forward to the lake," Zack said, making an attempt to get involved in the conversation. There was nothing like the sight of sunrise on the water. He wondered if it would still retain its magic for him. He privately doubted it.

There was forest on either side of the narrow road, and Zack slowed down to avoid any further potential accidents. When the vehicle passed over a bump in the road, he was thankful he had reduced his speed. He followed a faded green sign at a fork in the road and turned left.

Drifter's Folly Lodge, two miles, read the sign.

Good, Zack thought. He was ready to stretch his legs. Zack was six-foot-two, shorter than Will by less than an inch. The two friends looked a great deal alike. Both possessed straight jet-black hair. Zack's eyes were blue, and Will's were blue-green. In college people often mistook them for brothers. There was a hunger in Will's face that wasn't there in Zack's, which amounted to one difference between them.

"This place is really far out there," Dave said as he shoved a ball cap over his red hair.

"My phone has already lost service," Steve said. "What about the rest of you?"

"Mine seems to be holding on for the moment," Cole replied nervously. The busy student was practically joined at the hip to his smart-phone.

"Forget about your phones," Will said. "The farther we are from the civilized world, the easier it is to appreciate nature."

Zack agreed. Drifter's Folly was huge, and offered a variety of natural attractions. Aside from the standard lake, rivers, and forests, there were also mountains, canyons, and caves. They would try to explore as much as they could before the weekend was over.

The road turned onto a gravel path leading up a winding hill. The lodge materialized a few seconds later. Surrounded by a few trees, the spacious oak building was secluded from the outside world. The building was old, built on a massive stone foundation. A virtually abandoned parking lot boasted no more than four cars. The lot was fenced off, though Zack saw little reason for the security. He pulled into the lot and drove through one of the many empty spots.

"The place looks vacant," Cole said. Even Will looked surprised at the nearly empty lot.

Zack stared at the building a few moments longer before turning off the engine. The five men made their way out of the vehicle and into the sunlight.

"We might as well go inside," he said. "This will be our last chance to use a proper restroom for quite some time."

"You guys go ahead," Will said. "Dave and I will get the gear ready while you're gone." He stretched toward the hood and started unpacking.

Zack turned and walked in the direction of the lodge, followed by Cole and Steve. The hill was high enough they would have been able to see the highway if not for the forest.

He felt a chill when he entered the lodge. It was cooler than he expected. The wooden floor creaked beneath his weight.

"Hello?" Zack said, looking around for any sign of life. "Is anyone here?"

There was no response. Aside from some certificates and pamphlets, the entrance hall was bare. Steve saw a sign pointing to the restrooms and excused himself. Once Steve vanished, Zack found Cole staring at him.

"What's wrong?" he asked.

"I just wanted to make sure everything was okay," Cole said. "What happened back there, on the road? I didn't want to say anything before."

Zack tensed. He'd nearly forgotten about the brush with death that occurred as a result of his reminiscing. "Sorry about that. I was looking down at the map, and swerved a little off the road," he lied. "I didn't see the truck trying to pass me until it was almost too late."

"Okay. I just wanted to make sure."

They walked down the entrance hall, reading some of the certificates and plaques mounted on the walls. There was nothing that mentioned the origin of the park's name.

"I wonder how old this place is," Cole muttered as he looked around.

They passed a soda machine that looked like it predated their existence by several decades. There was a keepsake store just past the entrance hall to the right. Shadowy shelves were packed with stuffed bears, candy, and postcards. The dark room was obviously closed. Zack had a hard time believing the gift shop received a great deal of business. He peered through the glass window at one of the bears, which was somehow unnerving in the dark.

The stairs below led to a game room. Instead of taking the stairs, the two men continued into the main hall. The room was covered in trophy animals long ago stuffed by the taxidermist. Zack found himself staring into the eyes of a fox. He was surprised at how lifelike the dead animal remained.

Two desks loomed ahead. The plaque above one read *Drifter's Folly Registration,* and the other read simply *Security.* Both desks were vacant.

It's like we stepped into a ghost town, Zack thought.

Cole was still engaged with a towering stuffed bear. "Creepy." He reached out to touch the bear's snout.

"What do you think you're doing?" a stern voice demanded.

Cole jumped. Zack turned and saw an old man watching them

with an accusing gaze. The man looked ancient, like a stereotypical mountain man with a full beard and long white hair.

"Nothing," Cole blurted out, instinctively pushing up glasses that weren't there.

"We're just looking around," Zack said. "We're going camping and wanted to drop in and make ourselves known."

The old man's expression changed in an instant. "Camping, eh?" He smiled, revealing a toothy grin. "Name's Hickory Johnson. Haven't seen many campers recently."

"I'm Zack Allen, and this is Cole Wallace."

The old man took a step back, which put him between the two men and the registration desk.

"Y'all want a cabin? I've got some cheap rates."

Zack shook his head and Hickory's smile faded. He headed toward the registration desk.

"Well, here's a list of stuff to watch out for, park rules, and general guidelines to make sure ya'll stay safe." He handed the papers to Cole. "You fellers have any solar phones?"

"Cellular phones," Cole corrected.

"You won't be able to use solar phones out in the park. Bad reception and all that."

Zack nodded, having expected the news. Cole looked crestfallen.

Steve wandered into the room and spotted the three men standing there.

"Hi there," he said to Hickory. He admired a large pair of antlers adorning the wall before looking at Zack. "Anything I missed?"

"This is Mr. Johnson," Zack said. "He was just giving us some papers. Thanks for that, by the way."

"No problem," Hickory said, shaking his hand. The old man's grip was surprisingly strong.

"Did you say the phones wouldn't work?" Steve asked. Hickory nodded. "How can we reach you if there's a storm or something?" Steve tried to appear nonchalant, but Zack could tell he was a little nervous, even if he was reluctant to admit it. This was his first time camping, after all.

Hickory gestured to the empty security desk. A nameplate read *Ranger Austin Fields*. There were no pictures or papers visible on the desk, only a large number of stacked boxes. There was a dark office behind the desk labeled *Security* in bold letters.

"You're in good hands with Ranger Fields. He's been doing this for years."

"Where is Fields?" Steve asked lightly.

"Out and about, most likely. Haven't seen him yet today. Any other questions?"

Zack shook his head.

"Well, it was nice meeting you," Cole said. "Thanks for your help."

"We'd best be getting back to the others," Zack said. "Will and Dave will have unpacked everything by now." They walked back through the entrance hall and left the lodge.

"About time," Will said when they returned to the vehicle. "I thought it'd be noon before you finished in there. You guys ready to get rolling?"

"Definitely," Steve said.

The gravel road continued on a little farther. A trail loomed just beyond. According to the name on the sign, the trail was called Beggar's Road. It would probably take a few hours to reach the spot where they would set up camp. They'd stop for lunch before then.

Zack grabbed his pack while Cole handed out the maps. Dave shut the back of the van.

"Let's do this," Will said.

They started off in the direction of the trail. The trip had begun.

***

From the shade of the lodge, Hickory Johnson watched the five men start down the road through the window. The old man turned and retreated down the entrance hall. The floor was getting a little dusty. He made a mental note to clean up before turning in later.

His movements were slow, a symptom of the arthritis in his knees. He'd been part of Drifter's Folly for decades, and it was starting to show. Hickory caught a glimpse of himself in the glass window of the gift shop and didn't like what he saw. He'd always possessed a raw vitality, even at his age. Now Father Time was starting to catch up to him.

Time dealt him a cruel hand, just like his beloved park. The park's revenue had declined at a dangerous rate over the last eight years. Drifter's Folly operated in the red for the last five. The state was allocating budget funds elsewhere. There was talk of closing the park for good.

He glanced out the window one last time before returning to the registration desk. The five men had not yet vanished down the trail. He hoped they knew how lucky they were. If Drifter's Folly shut down, the scenic park would likely be lost forever.

His back turned, Hickory never saw the shadowy figure standing behind him. The figure silently raised a large pair of elk antlers from the wall and struck the old man in the back of the head. Hickory fell to the floor and heard something clatter to the ground beside him. He coughed and tried to crawl forward. A pair of strong arms grabbed his legs. Hickory tried to claw his way free, but his strength faded quickly. The figure seized the old man by the neck and finished his work. When he was done, he stashed Hickory Johnson's body in a closet and locked the door with the old man's keys. It would be days before the corpse was discovered. By then it would be too late.

The killer walked back to the main room and returned the antlers to the wall. He stood briefly in front of the window where Hickory had watched the five men wandering down the trail. The killer watched them too. The last of his guests for the weekend had arrived. What a weekend it would be.

He remained in the room, appreciating the lodge's décor. It was a tribute to death. He felt right at home. The killer knew he couldn't stay there forever. There was too much to do. Besides, he couldn't risk discovery at this point, not when the fun was about to begin. Too much time had elapsed since his last killing spree. The press called him 'The Hunter.' They actually weren't far from the truth.

He'd been ready to finish the old man earlier, but then the five men arrived. One of them came close to spotting him in the darkness. He could've killed the man there and then, but decided to let him live for the moment. The time wasn't right.

He hoped the campers would try to enjoy themselves while they could. Once night had fallen, they would know fear as never before, and then they would know death.

With that, the killer left the lodge and made his way into the forest.

The game was about to begin.

CHAPTER TWO

12:30 PM

TEARS STREAMED DOWN HER FACE. She stood rooted to the spot, either unable or unwilling to do what he'd asked. The all-too typical look of self-doubt reappeared on her face. In the past he would have been at the ready with a comforting word or a hug. Today was different.

Zack stared at her, daring her to meet his gaze. Lily averted her eyes and stared down at the floor. They stayed like that for minutes. Both wanted the moment to end, but took no further action. There was an air of finality in the kitchen. One way or another, things were never going to be the same.

Now Lily was shaking as well. Unlike his rage, her trembling came from fear and shame.

"Zack," she said one last time.

He cut her off.

"Get out," he repeated. "Just go." Until the last two words his voice had been steel. It broke at the end. Somehow that seemed to hurt her more than anything else he said.

When Lily bowed her head, her expression revealed defeat. She understood this was different from all the other times. What she'd done this time she could never take back. Zack looked past her. Behind her head, a framed photograph adorned the wall.

It was a reminder of better days.

"When are we planning on stopping for lunch?" Steve asked.

Zack stopped. The pack felt suddenly heavy against his back. He looked down at the path below. They'd been traveling just over two hours on the Beggar's Road, which led up a series of hills. It was an open trail through grassy fields. The heart of the forest was still miles away.

"We're probably halfway to the campsite," Will said. "Let's go a little farther before we stop to eat."

"It's already half-past noon," Cole replied. "There are some trees just down the hill. It'll be a good spot for some shade."

Steve shot Cole a relieved smile. Dave nodded in agreement, and Will reluctantly acquiesced.

"Okay, but let's try to do things quickly. There's a lot to do today, and every second counts. There will be plenty of time to relax later." The four men started down the hill. Will looked back at Zack. "You coming, buddy?"

"What?" Zack asked, startled. "Sorry," he said, gazing off into the distance. "I was distracted." Clutching the straps of his backpack, he joined the others and made his way toward the shade.

He didn't dream about Lily anymore. Zack was thankful for that. Maybe the counseling accomplished something after all. At the same time, what did sleeping soundly matter when he saw her even while he was awake? Even without the nightmares, he still had trouble sleeping.

The feelings were supposed to lessen with time. That's what everyone said. Only they were wrong.

"They're all wrong," he muttered.

Lunch was a large paper bag containing peanut butter and jelly sandwiches. Zack liberated some water bottles from his pack and tossed them to the others.

"Drink up," he said. "It's starting to get hot." That was a slight exaggeration. Although the air had warmed considerably since they started on the trail, the heat was nowhere near searing. Still, Zack could see how drenched in sweat Steve already was and worried he wasn't doing enough to keep himself hydrated.

"Peanut butter and jelly," Dave said ruefully to Will. "I thought you said he was a chef."

"Baker," Zack corrected as he sank his teeth into the sandwich. After a few hours of hiking, it tasted especially good. "There's a difference." So far Dave hadn't said anything particularly offensive, but the lack of gratefulness irritated Zack all the same.

"You should just be thankful someone else took the trouble to pack our lunches for us," Will said.

The group's chatter had given way to silence on the early leg of the trail. That suited Zack just fine. He was grateful for any opportunity not to share information about the current state of his life with his friends, not to mention Dave.

"Wow," Steve said, stretching his legs from where he sat on a log, "my legs are already sore."

Will and Dave laughed.

"That's not a good sign," Will said with a smile. "The real climb hasn't even started."

Steve's own smile faded. "Are you serious?"

Will glanced at his map. "These hills are just the beginning. This trail avoids the forest and leads up toward the cliffs. That's where we'll make camp."

Zack thought Steve tried to hide it, but he clearly looked crestfallen.

"Don't worry," Cole said quickly. "It'll all be worth it once we reach the top. You saw the pictures in the lodge. The lake will be down below it, and it'll be beautiful." He looked to Zack for support.

"Yeah," Zack said. "A real sight to behold."

He didn't sound particularly convincing. His heart wasn't in it. *What's wrong with you?* he asked himself. *Can't you even try to have a good time?*

Zack decided to make an effort to get his head out of the clouds and be a good sport. He wouldn't let his mood ruin the trip for everyone else.

"You should like the lake, Steve. You're a big swimmer, right?"

Steve nodded. Zack thought he remembered Steve mentioning his involvement in competitive swimming somewhere before, though he wasn't sure.

"If I have enough energy left to swim," Steve replied.

"When did all of you turn into a bunch of old women?" Will asked sarcastically. He slapped Zack on the back. "We'll show them how it's done."

Zack laughed. "I have to hand it to you, this place really is gorgeous." That much was true. They were only able to catch glimpses of what lay in store through the distant trees as they hiked, but he was already impressed. The trickle of a river sounded not far away. The sky was a vivid blue, and the land was green with the color of life.

"So, did you find out why the park is abandoned when you went inside the lodge?"

Zack shook his head. "Hickory didn't mention it. I figured it has to do with the time of year."

"That lodge gave me the creeps," Steve said. Zack didn't disagree, but was surprised to hear Steve express it in words. Lean and muscular, Steve didn't seem the worrisome type.

"Speaking of the lodge, make sure you keep your water bottles," Cole said. "The guidelines warn against littering."

Dave rolled his eyes. "Oh my, littering. Whatever will happen to us?" He shook his head. "I'm still waiting for this party to get started. Who brought the liquor?"

"Are you serious?" Cole asked. "Do you want to get dehydrated?" He took out his phone before sliding it back into his pocket.

"No service?" Zack asked. Cole shook his head sadly. "Then you're the last of us," he said. "From here out we're on our own."

As Zack started to pack his things away, he thought he heard something rustling in the bushes behind them.

He stood and peered into the forest. Of the other four campers, only Will noticed something had startled him. Zack was ready to turn back around when he thought he saw a silhouette partially concealed by a tree. The rustling sound stopped.

"Did you guys hear that?" he asked.

Before anyone could answer, the roar of an engine echoed in the distance. The others rose to their feet. The five men watched as a compact terrain vehicle drove up the trail, kicking up dust in its wake. The solitary driver behind the wheel seemed not to notice them. He wore a khaki-colored suit, sunglasses and a dark brown wide-brimmed hat. The driver sped past them.

The hikers stared at the path of dust as the engine roar died.

"Who was that?" Dave asked.

"I think it was the park ranger," Zack said, recalling the empty desk inside the lodge.

A few minutes later, the sound of the engine rose again. The vehicle returned over the hill and came to stop a few feet away from the campers.

"I almost didn't see you boys," the man said. He turned off the ignition and glanced in their direction. "Keeping cool?"

"Trying to, anyway," Steve said.

When the man stepped out of the vehicle, Zack immediately noticed the gun holstered at his side. The park ranger was a tall man, probably in his mid-forties. It was impossible to tell the color of his eyes given his sunglasses, but he had dark brown hair. The man's face was covered in stubble. Zack studied the patch on his uniform. It read *Park Ranger*.

The man held out his hand and Will shook it.

"My name is Austin Fields," he said. "I'm the Park Ranger at Drifter's Folly."

"We saw your plaque down at the lodge," Steve volunteered.

21

The ranger raised an eyebrow. "Did you? You boys didn't happen to run into old Hickory Johnson by any chance, did you?"

"Sure," Zack replied. "Why do you ask?"

"No reason," Fields answered. "He wasn't in the lodge when I arrived. He must have stepped out. It's just..." he trailed off.

Zack could tell he was uncomfortable about something. "What is it?"

Fields scratched at the growth on his chin. "Hickory rarely leaves early, and certainly not without leaving a note. His car was there too, which was odd."

"Maybe he went for a walk," Dave said.

The ranger nodded. "Could be. It just doesn't sit right with me. That's one of the reasons I'm glad I spotted you all on my way up the mountain."

Zack could tell the others were as curious as he was. Something was definitely going on at the park to make the ranger feel uneasy.

"Is everything all right?" he asked.

"I'm not sure," Fields said carefully. "We've been having some problems with poaching in the park. Over the last few days more than a few campers have reported being watched by a man in the forest."

"Like a stalker?" Steve asked. Fields nodded.

"I never spotted the man myself, but it's been on my mind. Ordinarily I wouldn't think anything of it, but the reports remind me of what happened in Texas just before the last Hunter killings."

"Hunter?" Zack's furrowed brow was evidence of his curiosity.

"You haven't heard?" Fields looked away, as if regretting bringing up the subject.

"He said killings," Steve said. His eyes were wide.

"Don't get worked up," the ranger said. "A couple of years ago in Texas, a group of campers were found dead in one of the state parks, murdered. The press called the killer 'The Hunter.' Apparently it wasn't the first time he'd killed."

"That sounds like some kind of a serial killer," Cole said with considerable skepticism.

Again, Fields nodded. "I only know about it because of the security measures we had to put in place after the killings, but from what I understand, it was big news at the time."

Zack studied the ranger's expression. The man was completely serious. His story sounded far-fetched at worst, paranoid at best. If there was a killer out there, it wasn't likely that he was lurking in Drifter's Folly. At the same time, Zack was hesitant to distrust the ranger's judgment.

"Do you think we should leave?" Steve asked.

Fields chuckled. "I doubt there's any need for that. You're more likely to run into a bear than some unhinged maniac. I just wanted you to be aware, that's all."

"A heads up isn't going to help if a serial killer comes knocking," Dave said.

Fields' eyes narrowed under his sunglasses. "That's why I stopped here." He returned to the terrain vehicle and grabbed a box. "I'm letting all the campers borrow these." He handed the group two walkie-talkies.

"How many others are out here?" Will asked, taking the devices. He handed one to Zack. "The parking lot was abandoned."

"At least three," the ranger answered. "A male and female couple, and one man on his own. They've already set up camp elsewhere. As for the few numbers, part of that could stem from the reports I told you about, though numbers have been dwindling for a while." Fields turned on his own walkie-talkie to demonstrate its use. "You've probably already discovered it for yourselves, but cellular phones don't work out here. These could save your life."

"Thanks," Zack said.

"I recommend turning them to channel twenty-three," the ranger added. "That's where I'll be listening if you need me. It seems to be the clearest channel. Again, you shouldn't need them.

I'm probably just being paranoid. If something—anything—does happen, I'll be here." Fields smiled reassuringly. The breeze drifted through the trees and gathered strength, rattling branches. The hikers fell silent for a moment.

"We appreciate it," Zack said finally.

The ranger looked over his shoulder into the forest.

"Well, that's all for now. I have to find the other campers before looking for Hickory. I'll try to check in with you boys in the morning." He opened the door to the terrain vehicle. "And boys?" he asked before he stepped inside. "Try to stay safe."

"Well," Dave said once the ranger was out of earshot, "that was certainly unsettling."

Zack frowned. For once he agreed with Dave. Even Will looked unsure of himself for a moment.

"What do you think, guys?" Steve asked. "Want to head back? It's not too late."

Will glared at him. "Don't even think about it. We didn't come this far to let some country park ranger scare us away with a few horror stories. Now get your stuff and let's go. We've wasted too much time here already."

Zack didn't agree with Will's wording, but his friend was right. It was silly to give up at the mere possibility of danger. Life was full enough of death on its own. He understood that better than anyone.

It was then that he remembered the figure he thought he saw in the forest behind them. Zack turned back and glanced near where the figure had been standing. There was nothing there.

I must have been imagining things, he thought. He hoisted his pack up against his back and walked back toward the trail. The others quickly caught up. Steve lagged behind, and Cole dropped back to keep him company.

"Nice pep talk back there," Zack said to Will. "Way to inspire the troops."

Will wore a frustrated look. "We were never like that, even when we were in college."

You can't blame Steve, Zack thought. *It's natural to be afraid of the unknown. That's part of the adventure.*

Awe was a double-edged sword. A storm could be both beautiful and terrible to behold at the same time. Nature had a mind of its own and didn't hesitate to remind them all too frequently. Zack couldn't count the number of times they'd encountered impossible weather in the past, not to mention smaller inconveniences like poison oak.

The forest loomed ever closer as they wandered down the path. Beggar's Road was the only trail that avoided the woods, but they would have time to explore the forest soon enough. The trail was the fastest way to reach the top of the Whispering Reach, the place where Will had decided they would make camp. According to the map, it was at the top of the cliff right above Dire Lake.

It didn't take Zack long to forget about the figure in the forest or Ranger Fields' words of caution. The five campers found themselves in awe of wonders of nature. Even Steve seemed to forget his struggles as they neared the cliff.

"There it is," Will said. He pointed to the towering rock landmark.

"Wow," Cole muttered. "That's impressive." Zack nodded. The roar of a waterfall echoed across the afternoon sky. A river materialized to their right. Zack consulted the map, which showed a tributary flowing into Dire Lake.

"Can I see that?" Dave asked. Zack handed him the map. There were three different rivers running through Drifter's Folly, each of which emptied into the lake.

Several minutes later, the Beggar's Road ended at a dirt trail not far from the cliff. The campers filed onto the unnamed path, one of many intersecting routes left off the map.

Zack glanced at Will. Drifter's Folly was larger than his friend led him to believe. This was their most ambitious undertaking yet. As Dave handed the map back to him, Zack frowned. He would have to remind Will to keep Dave and Steve close by. Even Cole might have problems if he was on his own. A park this size was no place to let a couple of neophytes wander around. It was easy to get lost. Once someone was lost, their prospects grew far worse. Dehydration, or in some cases predation, were serious problems. In retrospect, the small number of staffers employed by the park was unsettling.

The breeze died down and the day grew warmer as they turned east. Zack spotted a group of buildings strewn along the mountains looming in the distance.

"It looks like those are the cabins Hickory told us about," Cole said. "Too bad we're not staying there."

Steve looked wistfully at the cabins and down at the unforgiving ground. Zack knew what he was thinking; the same thought occurred to him as well. The hard earth was no help to his insomnia. Zack always found it strange how effortlessly some people managed to drift off after sliding into their sleeping bags. He, on the other hand, typically spent each night tossing and turning, alert to every sound outside the tent.

The cabins soon disappeared from view as they continued on their way. The journey up Whispering Reach took more time than anticipated. It wasn't long before the trees grew sparse, which left them fully exposed to the sun while they traveled higher and higher. Wiping sweat from his face, Zack drained another bottled water. He was looking forward to dropping his backpack and setting up camp. For some reason it bothered him that they still hadn't encountered any other campers, but he chose not to dwell on the subject.

After what seemed like an eternity, the five men reached the top of the cliff.

"Here we are," Will said with obvious pride. An exasperated

Steve took the opportunity to lower his gear and drop to a knee. Dave, the heaviest man in the group by about thirty pounds, appeared exhausted. He pulled off his cap and ran a hand through wet hair. Zack too dropped his pack as he walked toward the edge of the cliff.

He looked out over the precipice and surveyed the park. Directly below them, Dire Lake shimmered under the sunlight. The serene waters expanded in all directions. Zack closed his eyes and listened to the sound of the waterfall. When he opened them, Will was standing beside him.

"What do you think?"

"It's stunning," Zack answered.

He thought he'd lost the capacity to be amazed. He was happy to be wrong. Something about the peaceful park below evoked strong feelings of emotion from him. There was majesty mixed with sadness, a sense of loss he understood well.

Will slapped him on the back. "Let's get everything together. There'll be plenty of time for sightseeing later."

Zack nodded and went back to the others.

The group went to work, unpacking the equipment in their bags under Will's guidance.

"We can put the tent over there," he said while motioning toward a cluster of trees near the slope of the cliff.

"The regulations say we can build a fire," Cole said.

"We were going to anyway," Will replied. Cole looked at him reproachfully. "What? Like Ranger Fields was going to stop us." He shook his head. "You think he's ever actually fired that gun?"

Steve was standing close to the trees, his back turned to the rest of them. Zack froze. Steve was staring down at something on the ground. The others noticed and looked in Steve's direction.

Steve gripped his nose. It looked as if he was about to vomit. When Zack reached him, the smell of death filled the air.

"That's gross," Dave muttered.

There was a decaying corpse lying in the hot sun. Covered in flies, it was impossible to determine how long the animal's body had been there.

"What is it?" Steve asked.

"Probably a possum," Will said.

"It's too big to be a possum," Cole replied.

"Something did this," Steve said. "Do you think it was a coyote?"

"That's another reason we're building a fire," Will said. "It'll keep predators away."

Zack wasn't entirely sure it was a predator that had killed the rotting creature. "Look at its chest," he said. The animal's torso had been ripped apart. Its heart had been torn out.

Dave looked disgusted. "You sure picked a great spot for the tent," he said to Will. He lifted his foot and attempted to kick the corpse off the cliff. The kick wasn't strong enough, and the carcass instead landed a few feet from their tent. There was something callous about the way Dave kicked the animal that caused the others to look at him with disgust. Dave shrugged and kicked the corpse a second time. Blood stained the tip of his boot as he drew it back. Zack watched the bloodied carcass careen through the air and vanish in the water below.

"Okay, we need two people to stay here and set up the tent," Will said. "The rest of us will gather some firewood from the forest."

"I'll stay," Dave volunteered. "I don't feel like doing anymore walking for a while."

"Cole and Steve, you two can join me in the woods," Will said. "Zack, you stay with Dave."

Zack wanted to protest. The prospect of being left alone with Dave wasn't appealing to him in the slightest. He didn't particularly care for how Dave had treated the dead animal, his mocking comments earlier on the road, or his snide attitude either. It didn't help that Zack already found himself on edge. He hadn't been around the same people for an extended period of time in several months. Only a few hours into the trip, and he was already wearing thin.

"We should be able to do this quickly enough," he said once the others were gone. "Then we can relax until everyone else gets back."

"Suits me," Dave replied. "I'm just glad I didn't get stuck with Steve."

Zack didn't reply. Instead, he focused on laying out all the parts of the large tent. Dave had trouble following his instructions, and it took them a while to get everything in order.

Dave hit his finger while hammering in a stake. He swore loudly, and the sound echoed off the cliff. Zack finished with his stake and moved onto the next.

"You're doing it wrong," Zack said reluctantly as they continued. "Let me help."

Dave scowled at him. "I don't need your help."

Zack threw his hands up in the air. "Whatever."

His tone apparently conveyed his annoyance, because Dave looked up at him. "Did I say something wrong?" he demanded.

"It's nothing," Zack answered. "It's been a while since I've been out like this, that's all."

Dave looked at him funny, like he couldn't comprehend what Zack said. "That's right. Will mentioned you having problems adjusting to something. It'll be all right," Dave said. "Just give it time."

Zack froze. He remembered the last time he heard those words. "Don't you ever say that to me again."

Dave stood and threw down his stake. "What's your problem, man?" He walked up to Zack until their chests were practically touching.

"You should shut up about things you don't understand," Zack said. He shoved Dave forcefully, and the big man stumbled back.

"Psycho," Dave whispered under his breath.

That was enough for Zack. He punched Dave hard in the face. The blow sent the heavy man to the ground. Blood poured from Dave's nose. He looked up at Zack with disbelief in his eyes.

Zack stood there, looking down at Dave. His left fist was still clenched tightly shut. He glanced at the fist and back at Dave. As his blood cooled, he realized he'd completely lost control of his temper.

"Zack?" Cole said from behind them. Zack turned and saw Cole and Will climbing the slope. Steve materialized seconds later. Cole looked from Zack to Dave.

"Don't," Zack said, storming off in the direction of the woods. "Just don't."

Cole started to follow him, but Will grabbed his arm. "Let me talk to him."

Cole nodded and exchanged looks with Steve before walking over to Dave. "Are you okay?" he asked the big man, helping him up.

"I think so," Dave said. "What the heck is that guy's deal?"

"He's going through a tough time," Cole answered reluctantly. "His ex-girlfriend died a few months ago." Steve's expression softened, though Dave remained angry. Cole peered off into the distance.

"She committed suicide."

CHAPTER THREE

3:05 PM

LILY CAST A LAST FURTIVE glance in his direction before finally walking away. When she reached the hallway, Lily stopped at the door. Zack stood in the kitchen doorway, waiting for her to leave.

"For what it's worth," she said, still not meeting his eyes, "I am sorry."

As her hand gripped the doorknob, he spoke again. His voice was cutting.

"I wish I'd never met you."

Much like what she had done to him, they were words he would never get back.

She turned and fled into the night. The door slammed shut behind her.

Zack remained standing behind the kitchen counter. His knees were wobbly. His gaze returned to the photo on the wall behind where Lily had stood. He suddenly found himself holding it in his hands. In the photograph, the two of them were standing together just outside his bakery. Surely the smiles on their faces were lies. At the moment, he couldn't remember ever being happy.

In the picture, they were holding a cake he made for her. He gripped the picture tightly as he read the words etched in icing.

"Forever."

Zack hurled the picture against the wall. Glass shattered, and the picture fell to the floor.

"You can't hide forever," Will said loudly, his voice echoing off the trees. Without looking, Zack could feel his friend's gaze seek him out.

"What?" Zack asked. He turned around and watched Will make his way across the fallen leaves.

"You heard me. I know everything's been rough on you. That doesn't mean you should lock yourself away forever. You aren't the only one who cared about her."

"I get out," Zack said defensively.

"The bakery doesn't count. How long has it been since you've done something for yourself?"

Zack shook his head. The honest answer was one he didn't plan on voicing. *Not since the funeral,* he thought silently.

The two men stood quietly for a few moments, listening to the sounds of nature.

"You really knocked Dave to the ground, didn't you?" Will asked with a grin.

"Don't ask me to apologize."

"I'm not Cole. Dave probably had it coming."

"Did you tell him I was having problems?"

Will's smile faded, and he hesitated. "Those aren't the exact words I used," he said reluctantly before looking away.

Zack's eyes narrowed at his friend. The anger rose again, unbidden. He wasn't going to start throwing punches again, but that didn't mean he was feeling particularly benevolent toward his old roommate at the moment.

It wasn't right of him to share that, he thought. He could imagine the careless way with which Will probably imparted the private information. Will was extremely self-centered, which meant he experienced difficulty with traits like empathy and discretion.

Zack sighed and realized blaming Will wouldn't do him any

good. His anger at the world was enough to keep him functioning. It wasn't enough to fill the black hole inside him. His counselor described the anger as a coping mechanism, a way he didn't have to blame himself. Zack wasn't sure about that, because he did blame himself.

"Sorry if I told Dave something I shouldn't," Will said. "Sometimes I don't think about how my actions affect other people."

The surprising candor of his self-assessment took Zack by surprise. Perhaps his old friend was maturing after all.

"It's okay," he said. "I guess we're all guilty of that from time to time."

"Well, if that's that, we should get back to camp. There's still enough time to start exploring before sundown."

He turned to go. Zack stood still for a moment, watching his friend. He wanted to desperately to tell Will, to tell anyone, why he blamed himself for Lily's death.

"Will," he said.

His friend glanced back at him. "Yeah? Was there something else?"

Zack choked on the words. He couldn't do it. He shook his head and joined Will in the march up the slope. The secret would remain his alone. It wasn't that he didn't want to confess. He did, more than anything. There were many opportunities in the past, starting with the funeral. He'd come close to telling Cole before. Even Zack's counselor sensed he was holding something back.

Most of his friends knew he blamed himself for Lily's death, but no one knew the full story. Zack wasn't sure why he couldn't share what happened between them. Maybe keeping the past buried was his way of protecting Lily's memory, his way of seeking forgiveness for the words he'd said.

The others were waiting for them when they returned. Dave looked at him coolly. Zack could see a trace of blood under his nostrils. He immediately felt guilty.

"I shouldn't have done that," he finally said. The rage told him not to apologize, but he knew it was the only way to clear the air. "Are we cool?"

Everyone looked at Dave, waiting for his response. He bit his lip and nodded.

"Sure."

Zack could tell Dave didn't mean it. He was probably reacting to pressure from the group. He considered extending his hand to the redhead, but the gesture felt empty and awkward. It was probably best to act like nothing happened.

"So what now?" Cole asked, changing the subject. Zack noticed lingering concern in his eyes whenever Cole looked at him. Unlike Will, Cole had picked up on Zack's mood when they were inside the lodge. Now Zack regretted not confiding in him.

Will cleared his throat. "We can take the trail leading back through the Red Pine Forest, or we can take Dead Man's Drop to the other side of the cliff and go past the lake."

"We've already seen Red Pine on the way," Dave said. "Even if we didn't go through it. Besides, there's plenty of forest nearby the lake."

"I think I could use a swim after all," Steve added. "I vote lake."

Zack agreed with the others. The lake was beautiful, and there was a cave close by he wanted to explore. "Is anyone up for Shallow Water Cave? The map mentions it floods in the summer, but we should be all right this time of year."

"Count me in," Cole said. He tossed Zack one of the flashlights. The campers left their gear behind in the tent. Before they abandoned the campsite, Zack grabbed the two-way radio Fields gave him just in case.

A thin layer of soil covered in jagged rocks, Dead Man's Drop proved every bit as challenging to descend as the name suggested. The steep incline was nothing like the slope they'd taken up Whispering Reach. Zack considered it fortunate they didn't have to make the trip with their backpacks. When he came close to slipping several times, Zack peered over the ledge. A fall from such a height was more than unappealing.

By the time they reached the valley below, everyone was wiped out. Steve wasted no time changing into his shorts and jumping into the lake. Dave joined him. The large man was covered in sweat. The three friends watched them swimming from the shore, cloaked in the shade of Whispering Reach. The sun glistened brightly off the water's surface.

Steve paddled to the bank. "Are you guys coming in?"

"Not me," Zack answered. "I'm not getting wet today."

Cole nodded in agreement. "Besides, we should probably get started looking for that cave." As Zack took out his map, Cole looked at Will. "What about you?"

"I'll stay here with these two," he answered while dangling his feet in the water. "There's a trail that leads by one of the rivers not far from here. When they're finished swimming, I want to check it out."

A flock of ravens rose from the forest not far away. The birds ascended into the cloudless sky, passing over the campers as they sailed toward the cliff.

"Okay," Cole said. "When should we meet up?"

"Seven sounds about right," Will replied. "That gives us enough time to get back to camp before sunset. We'll all meet here."

The group split up, and the pair walked into the forest. It didn't take long to find the path leading to Shallow Water Cave. A faded wooden sign with a painted red arrow pointed them in the right direction. Zack was glad Cole chose not to mention what happened with Dave. As they neared the outskirts of the cave, his attention turned to the task at hand.

"Watch your step," he said as he stepped into the entrance, which was narrower than he'd expected. "You might want to duck," he added.

Once they moved inside, the cave began to expand. The air

was musty and cold, and the earth was damp. Zack flipped on his flashlight. Behind him, the beam of Cole's flashlight illuminated the cave.

"Wow," Cole said, stepping around a column. "It's even bigger than I thought." After inhaling a lungful of dust, he sneezed loudly. "It smells awful in here." The echo filled the cave. Zack suspected Cole was glad he wasn't wearing his glasses. There was dust everywhere.

"Look up there," Zack said. He trained his beam on the ceiling. "Bats." There were clusters of the flying mammals hanging from the cave ceiling. Cole's eyes widened nervously.

As the two campers advanced farther within the cave, neither noticed a body leaning against the stone wall in the dark recesses of the cavern. The figure was slumped against the wall, its lower torso submerged in a deep pool of water. Unlike the animal carcass on the cliff, the remains were, without question, human.

***

Dry leaves crunched underneath his boots. Austin Fields cast a look back at his all-terrain vehicle before moving farther into the woods. The continuous expanse of the forest was a labyrinth of sorts. Despite the park's size, he was far too experienced to get lost. The same couldn't be said of the campers who frequented Drifter's Folly. After several minutes, the ranger reached a tent close to the river.

"Hello?" he asked in an attempt to alert anyone in the vicinity to his presence. There was no answer. The ranger stared down at the tent, which was rather clumsily put together. The zipper wasn't pulled up all the way, which gave him a glimpse into the contents inside. The tent was empty. It seemed too small to belong to the men he'd run into on the Beggar's Road.

It was a poor location for a tent. The bare earth was wet beneath his feet. The tent was covered in mud, some of which had already started to dry. Fields searched for any clue as to the whereabouts of the tent's owner. He found nothing. There was a single sleeping bag inside, indicating a sole occupant. Whoever set up the tent was probably out exploring alone. It would be light outside for several hours, so that wouldn't be much of a problem for the time being. If the camper didn't return before sundown, it would be a different matter.

Fields came this far to deliver one of the two-way radios to the mystery camper and share the message he'd conveyed to the five men headed for Whispering Reach. Now it looked like he'd made the trip for nothing. He wanted to wait for the camper to return, but there were other matters requiring his attention. Retrieving a pen from his pocket, the ranger scrawled a hasty message on the back of one of his spare maps. He unzipped the tent farther and lowered the note inside, along with the walkie-talkie, inside. Hopefully, the camper would see the note whenever he or she returned.

Fields started back across the wet earth. The river roared in the background, its current stronger than usual. A muffled sound echoed through the trees to his west. The ranger stopped. Perhaps the camper had returned after all.

"Hello?" he called.

The whistling of the breeze was the only reply. Fields stared into the forest. He felt uneasy. Shadows rotated as the trees swayed in the wind, spinning like ballroom dancers.

"Is someone there?" The ranger's hand instinctively reached for his sidearm.

The forest remained still. Fields sighed and released his grip on the weapon.

***

Rodney Crowe watched Fields standing in the open woods. For a moment, he thought the ranger sensed him. The killer dismissed the thought instantly, as he was too well hidden. Crowe saw the ranger's eyes flicker down to his gun.

You can't hit what you can't see, he silently remarked.

After a prolonged silence, Fields turned and headed back to his all-terrain vehicle. Crowe remained concealed in the forest, watching until the ranger passed out of sight. It was almost too easy. Crowe quietly traced Fields' steps until he found the abandoned tent. The ranger's instincts were correct. He was right to try and alert the camper who'd pitched his tent near the river. With the current as strong as it was, it would be difficult for the camper to find refuge if attacked. Conversely, it would be child's play to slit the man's throat when the time came.

The killer slowly zipped open the front of the tent. His eyes scanned the note Fields left behind. Crowe decided to leave the note in place. The unwitting victims who had descended on Drifter's Folly that weekend needed all the advantages they could get. The game was about to begin, and everyone was playing. Even Ranger Austin Fields.

Crowe didn't want to be caught standing around when the tent's owner returned. It wasn't that he feared a confrontation with the man. He would come for the camper before the night was over. For now, the timing was wrong. Now was the time to anticipate. It was an emotion to savor.

His lips were smeared with blood where he'd bitten into the fox's heart. No matter where he killed, the ritual was always the same. He would stalk the park for a few weeks, learning the lay of the land. If he was in the mood for a challenge, he might allow himself to be spotted. When the night of hunting approached, he would kill a forest animal and consume a piece of its heart before beginning his work. The ritual held significant meaning for him. Everything was prey for something else. The only real way to achieve power in the world was in becoming a predator.

The five campers on the Beggar's Road had been headed in the direction of Whispering Reach. If they stopped at the cliff, they might find the carcass. The thought pleased him. Crowe remembered the man with the black hair who almost spotted him in the forest. Large groups were always more fun to hunt. The dynamic was exceptionally interesting to watch. As circumstances became more desperate, the hunted always reverted to a more primal state. This would help them survive—for a time. Before the night was over, however, everyone in the park would die. It was always the same.

Crowe licked the blood on his lips in anticipation. There were only a few more hours left.

CHAPTER FOUR

5:46 PM

I T WAS THE DAY OF Lily's funeral. Although Zack's sense of betrayal hadn't abated over the months preceding her death, the bitterness ebbed with each day. He'd just started learning to live again in a world without her in it, and then that world came crashing down around him.

Thunder ripped through silence as the casket was closed. Zack could only watch expressionlessly. Rain pelted him from above. He was standing as close to the family as he dared. No one knew all that passed between the couple, but he suspected Lily's parents were aware they parted on bad terms.

When it was over, Lily's mother found him. Mrs. Sanders looked like she'd aged ten years since he last saw her. A black umbrella shielded her body from the rain. Despite being almost a foot taller than the demure woman, Zack couldn't shake the feeling she was looking down at him.

"You," she said darkly. Her eyes flashed in concert with another round of thunder.

"I'm sorry for your loss," he managed to say. The words rang hollow.

"She did this because of you," Mrs. Sanders said. Having spotted her, the woman's husband tried to pull her away from Zack. She broke free of his grip and looked Zack dead in the eyes. He felt compelled to say something, to offer some kind of explanation.

"I never wanted this to happen."

"Then why didn't you save her?" Her tone changed from accusatory to pleading. "She was drowning and you cut her off. You left her alone."

"There was nothing I could do."

This was the lie that was to become the first of many he would tell himself.

The rage reappeared in her eyes. It was a feeling he would come to know well in the months ahead.

"Of course not. You're too much of a survivor for that."

Those words stayed with him, partially because she was right. In that respect, he was always different from Lily.

He might've never met Lily Sanders if not for an impromptu phone call from Will. He was in college at the time, about to complete a degree in business administration. Zack's head was buried in his notes when his cell phone went off. It was Will. He was in a bar—one of his many regular haunts—and in serious need of a driver to take him back to campus. It wasn't the first time one of Will's nights of fun ended this way, and Zack seriously considered letting him find the way back to school on his own. For some reason he decided to pick his friend up in the end, swearing it would be the last time he allowed Will to take advantage of him. By the time Zack arrived at the bar, Will had changed his mind. He no longer wanted to leave. After persuading Zack to stay, he returned to his preoccupation with hitting on women.

That was when Zack saw her. One of the women in Will's path of havoc caught Zack's eye. When they were together, Lily often claimed she looked plain, but that night she appeared captivating and enticing. Zack struck up a conversation with her and apologized for Will's conduct in advance. They hit it off almost immediately. Will later complained that he intended to flirt with Lily all along, and that Zack swooped in too early. Zack found this perspective comical at best. He'd lost track of the number of girls he'd been interested in who Will moved in on over the years.

Cole's footsteps echoed in the cave, and again Zack's recollection ended abruptly.

"This place is amazing," Cole said.

Zack silently agreed. He lowered himself from the ledge and dropped to the ground below.

"Watch out for the pool of water," he said, shining the flashlight so Cole could see his way to the bottom. Faint light from the beam glinted off dark water. The farther they went, the more water seeped inside the cavern. The cave seemed to go on forever.

Zack waded through the water. At least twice he thought he felt something swim past his foot. He hoped it wasn't a snake. When he was almost up to his knees in water, Cole suggested they head back.

"What time is it?" Zack asked. Between exploring and reminiscing, he'd lost track of time. Cole removed his phone from his pocket. "You're still carrying that thing around?" He laughed.

"I can't live without it," Cole admitted sheepishly. "It's almost quarter till six."

Zack turned around. Part of him wanted to keep exploring the cave, but the water was too deep to go much farther anyway.

"All right," he said. "If we hurry, we'll still have time to take another trail back to Dire Lake."

The pair waded in the direction they came. Zack scaled the ledge first before helping Cole over the top. They walked until the light appeared outside the cave's entrance. Zack held his hand in front of his face so his eyes could readjust to the bright sun. He switched the flashlight off and put it away.

"Want some water?" Cole asked, extending a water bottle.

"Thanks," Zack said. He took the bottle and popped the top. "That probably tastes better than cave water."

Cole laughed. "That's the first joke I've heard you tell in a while." Zack didn't know how to respond, so he took a drink and kept silent. "How are you doing, man?"

"What do you mean?" Zack asked reluctantly.

"Just checking in. We haven't seen much of each other lately."

Aside from a dinner he'd tried to back out of, it was true.

"Sorry about that. I've been pretty wrapped up in things at work."

"You know you can tell me anything." Coming from someone else, the words would have sounded trite. Zack knew Cole was sincere. That didn't make it any easier to open up.

He shook his head. "I'm angry all the time now," he admitted. "You saw what I did to Dave."

Cole's eyes narrowed. "You're a good person. Don't let regret make you bitter."

Zack sighed. "What else can I do?"

"You've got to forgive whoever hurt you," Cole said, "and allow yourself to be forgiven."

His meaning was plain. Cole had invited Zack to church for weeks after Lily's funeral. Zack came up with a new excuse each week until he thought his friend finally took the hint.

"I know," he said. He gave Cole an encouraging pat on the back. "Thanks for being there. Now what do you say we hit the trail?"

The two resumed the trail that led toward Dire Lake. Cole didn't mention Lily again. Zack wished everyone would stop bringing her up. It wasn't like he didn't think about her enough as it was.

While the pair ventured deeper into the forest, Zack's thoughts returned to Lily. He'd been smitten with her after only a few dates. She was a talented artist who moved halfway across the country to pursue her goals. In her spare time she worked as a waitress at a café he frequented with Will. Lily was short and thin with a boundless supply of energy—most of the time. As his feelings for her grew, Zack slowly discovered his flighty but fun girlfriend possessed another side. At times she became introverted, insecure, and depressed. He suspected she suffered from some type of imbalance. Lily refused outright to be tested for any disorder.

Eventually Zack stopped pressing the issue. Whatever her flaws, he came to love her deeply. So he tried to do what he could to lift her spirits when she was in the dumps. She needed him. Although their relationship had its share of ups and downs, they remained committed to each other, or so he thought.

They were going through one of their rough patches the night she gave him the news. Zack was working late at the bakery and hadn't expected to see Lily when he returned home. He braced himself, hoping she wasn't there for another irrational argument. If only. Lily proceeded to confess that she'd spent the night with someone else. Zack never learned the identity of the man from Lily, and now he probably never would.

His heart was broken.

"It was a mistake," she said. "I was lonely. He was there for me."

All the words ran together. He was confused, unable to respond. When she tried to apologize, the anger welled up inside him. Zack kicked her out of his life. He never suspected she would try to hurt herself. It wasn't something he could comprehend. One of the doctors theorized the attempt on her life was a plea for help gone horribly wrong. To Zack, the intent didn't matter. She'd been reaching out for help, and he rejected her.

He felt no guilt for breaking up with her. His remorse came from everything that followed. The calls he left unanswered. The emails he deleted. So when Mrs. Sanders said he was a survivor, the comment stung. Zack felt he sacrificed Lily's well being for his own peace of mind. After investing so much energy into being her boyfriend, he wasn't willing to be the friend she needed.

When the funeral was over, he stood alone in the rain. He felt lost. There was nothing and no one to cling to. Even his friends seemed distant. Zack might have found solace in his faith, but God became someone else for him to blame.

The evening sky darkened as they made their way down the winding trail.

"We could hike for miles from here and still not make it back to the highway," he said. They were completely immersed in nature. He used to live for this. Now he wasn't sure how he felt.

"No thanks," Cole said. "I'll stick to a short hike and roasted marshmallows back at the tent."

Zack licked his lips. Marshmallows sounded good.

"What's that?" Ahead, something gleamed under a pile of leaves. Picking up a walking stick, Zack prodded the pile. Suddenly, a metal trap concealed underneath snapped shut.

Cole's eyes widened. "We almost stepped on that! Someone left that here on the path."

Zack frowned. "I don't think it was left here for us."

He bent down and brushed the leaves away. The enormous trap was large enough to break bone. The trap's sharp metal teeth could easily rip into flesh. "It looks like a bear trap to me. Fields did mention the park has had trouble with poachers recently." Even so, if they'd stepped into the trap, the result would be the same.

"What's a bear trap doing out here? I didn't even know there were bears in these woods."

Zack didn't have an answer for him. Something about the way the trap was concealed was troubling.

"I don't know," he said, "but I suggest we keep our eyes open on the way back to the lake."

***

Will checked his watch. Zack and Cole were running late. He decided to cross over to Shatter Creek Trail to save time.

"This way," he said. "It'll take us closer to the lake." Steve and Dave followed, though both moved at a slower pace than Will preferred.

The thick forest became sparse as they started on the new trail.

Shatter Creek flowed nearby, trickling steadily into Dire Lake. Will saw several large fish swimming through the clear water when they drew closer. Permit or no permit, he wasn't going to let this opportunity pass him by. He made a mental reminder to return to the creek with his fishing rod the next day.

Above, the yellow sun turned a dark orange. Will saw a boat ramp extending into the water on the bank. Water rushed over the small ramp, which was constructed from round, black logs. The ramp floated up and down against the current, looking like a miniature dock. An abandoned canoe was tied to the ramp by a rope. There were no paddles in sight. He wondered how long the canoe had been sitting in the water. From the looks of things, it was likely there a while.

Whispering Reach was visible from the bank. Clouds filled the once clear sky. Evening was well on its way, and Will increased his pace.

"You guys coming or what?"

He was beginning to lose his patience. The ragtag group of campers wasn't what he initially envisioned. Steve expressed enthusiasm when Will invited him. Will assumed, given his friend's past athleticism, that Steve would be a natural camper. Instead, the opposite was true. Inviting Steve was a mistake, and Dave too. Dave knew how to party, which was one of the reasons Will enjoyed his company. Unfortunately, Will underestimated the degree to which Dave's caustic personality grated against Zack.

Zack was still raw. The more he thought about it, the more irritated Will became. He'd done all this on Zack's behalf. The least the guy could do was show a little appreciation. Will went out of his way to be there for Zack when Lily died. Zack made it abundantly clear he wanted to be alone. That suited Will just fine. He was looking for a good time. Babysitting was for someone like Cole. Besides, Zack's days of self-pity were bound to run out eventually. That was why Will organized the trip to Drifter's Folly.

Enough time had passed since the funeral. It was time for Zack to start being fun again.

"What's that ahead?" Dave asked. The three men reached what looked like a rest area. There were several long wooden tables atop a concrete surface. A roof with black shingles mounted on poles protected the tables from the elements. There was a plaque affixed to the beam under the roof. *Recreation*, read the faded white letters.

"It doesn't look like anyone's been here in a while," Steve muttered. Will nodded in agreement.

An empty sand volleyball court loomed next to the creek. The net was barely intact, and there was no ball in sight. Two tires hung suspended from rusted iron chains fastened to a tree. Absent a rider, the tires swung to and fro in the breeze. There was a basketball backboard and rim on the other side of the tables, missing a net. The courts and tables appeared out of place in the naturalistic park.

"Look," Steve said. "Here's a horseshoe pit. Too bad we don't have any horseshoes."

Will stepped underneath the roof. Dry leaves covered the cement floor. He ran his hand over one of the wooden tables. Dozens of names were etched into the tables, all by people likely never to see them again. None of the dates carved into the table that were within the decade. Overall, the site was in bad shape. New signs of disrepair were evident around every corner.

"Here's a payphone," he said, stepping back onto the soil. "I wonder if it works."

His change was back inside his pack at the campsite.

A noise echoed behind him. Will felt goose pimples rise on his arms. Dave and Steve were in his line of sight. So what was making the noise coming from the pavilion?

He turned around slowly. A raccoon scrambled out of a trashcan, a crumb of bread protruding from its mouth. The scavenger looked him over and bounded through the volleyball court before scampering into the bushes.

"It looks like we aren't the only ones here after all," Dave said.

"What do you mean?" Steve asked.

"Someone's been here recently." He pointed to part of a sandwich left behind by the raccoon. The sandwich was fresh. Will studied the remains for a moment. The day grew darker.

"That's enough time for resting," he said. "Let's get back on the trail."

Exploring the seedy recreational area was a nice diversion, but the place was starting to give him the creeps. Will knew he wasn't alone. The others were obviously spooked when they left the lodge. Ranger Fields' story hadn't done anything to make that better.

The snapping of dry grass sounded ahead. Will rounded the corner, expecting another animal. Instead, he found himself face-to-face with a stranger. The man eyed him suspiciously as Will's two friends reached his side. Will noticed the two-way radio strapped to the man's belt. He recognized it as one of the units from Fields. A blonde woman stepped through the brush and nearly jumped when she spotted the three strangers.

"Sorry for scaring you," Will offered apologetically.

"No harm done," the man said. "Are you all right, honey?"

The woman nodded, still watching them.

"If it makes you feel any better, you gave me quite a start." Will smiled warmly. She was probably in her early thirties and moderately attractive. "I'm Will, by the way." He gestured to the others. "These are my friends, Dave and Steve. You're the first campers we've seen since we arrived."

"Us too," the man replied. He was stout, several inches shorter than Will, with brown hair and a goatee. "How long have you been here?"

"Just today," Will said. "We arrived this morning."

"We've been here for two days," the woman said. "I'm Beth."

"And I'm Ron," the man said. They shook hands. "So, where are you from?"

"Ohio," Will answered. "I found the place online. You two come here often?"

Beth shook her head. "It was a surprise," she said. Ron beamed at her, but Beth didn't seem quite as excited. Will picked up on the expression.

Ron's own expression changed. "None of you heard a gunshot earlier by any chance, did you?"

Dave shook his head. "Not us."

"Why would someone have a gun out here?" Steve asked. He looked worried.

Ron shrugged. "We thought it might be a poacher. We radioed Ranger Fields about it."

"What did he say?" Steve asked.

"He said it didn't come from him and that he'd check into it."

Will stepped forward. "Well, you can rest assured it wasn't us. Or the other two in our group."

Ron looked at Beth. "See, honey? Everything's okay." He glanced back at the others. "She's been a little jumpy since we met Fields."

"He seems to have that effect on people," Will replied. "I've been expecting someone to jump out at me all day. That's why I reacted the way I did when I ran into you." He rested a hand on Beth's shoulder. "No hard feelings?" he asked with a wink.

She shook her head. Will squeezed her shoulder ever so slightly, and Ron frowned a little.

"We'd probably better head back," Will said finally. "We're camped up at Whispering Reach if you want to drop by." He stared at Beth as he said the words.

"That could be fun. We'll think about it," Ron said, in a tone that implied such an idea was the furthest thing from his mind. The pair waved goodbye and continued walking in the direction of the recreation area. Will cast a glance back at Beth and grinned.

"I know what you're thinking," Dave said with a smile.

"I bet you don't," Will said, chuckling.

Steve didn't join in the laughter. There was still a look of worry on his face.

"Where do you think the gunshot came from?" he asked as they neared the end of the trail.

Will sighed. "I think Ron was probably right. It was a poacher. Like Fields said, Drifter's Folly has had problems with illegal hunters in the past." He looked at Steve. "There's no need to be worried about anything. Even if there was a psychopath hiding in the woods somewhere, there are five of us. In a park this size, there are thousands of places to hide." He held out the two-way radio. "Don't forget," he added, "we've got these."

The words sounded comforting, and Steve relaxed. Despite his speech, Will wasn't so sure. He kept his doubts to himself, but running into Ron and Beth did little to put him at ease. When they first met Fields, Will suspected the ranger was toying with them by sharing the story of the Texas murders. If the ranger told the same thing to the couple on the trail, that meant he was probably serious. That didn't mean Fields wasn't paranoid, though it did add new weight to his words of caution.

Zack and Cole were waiting for them at the end of the trail.

"Nice timing," Cole said. "We've only been here for a few minutes."

"You guys have fun?" Zack asked.

Will nodded. "The rapids on the other side of the lake are intense. Should make for some great rafting, if we can find a boat."

"I think there was a rental area at the back of the lodge that had some rafting boats," Zack mentioned.

Reunited, the group began climbing Dead Man's Drop. The ascent was more difficult than the way down. Even Will was worn out. By the time they reached the cliff, he was nearly ready to collapse.

"I might have to sleep in tomorrow," Cole said. "The ground probably won't feel so bad tonight." He took a seat in the shade next to Zack. Steve walked over to the tent to change into shorts and a t-shirt.

"I'm famished," Dave said.

It was the perfect time for dinner. Will went through the supplies next to the tent and removed a pack of hot dogs and some buns. The temperature had dropped considerably since their hike from the lodge that afternoon.

"I'll help with the fire," Zack volunteered. Will tossed his former roommate a lighter and scrounged around his pack for paper plates and condiments. His stomach roared with hunger.

"See anything cool while you were out there?" Will asked. He tried to keep his mind occupied while they waited for the fire to start. The sun had almost disappeared.

"Now that you mention it, we did find a bear trap." The growing fire crackled with energy. Zack took a step back.

Will raised an eyebrow. "In the cave?"

"On the trail. Someone hid it under a pile of leaves. Either of us could have stepped on it."

Will made a pained expression. "Ouch. Maybe the poacher set it up." He could see the question form on Zack's lips. "We met up with a pair of campers who heard a gunshot. They thought it came from the poacher Fields mentioned."

"Should we be worried?"

"Fields told them he was going to look into it. If there was an emergency, we'd know."

The fire glowed brightly in the darkening sky.

"Come on over!" Zack hollered to the others. "The fire's ready."

The campers took turns cooking hot dogs and marshmallows in the fire. Will passed around a few bags of chips, and the group sat around the fire to eat.

"That tastes good," Steve said. "You know, that wasn't so bad for my first time hiking."

"Let's see how you feel when you wake up tomorrow," Dave said. Everyone laughed, including Steve.

"So, what were the campers you met like?" Zack asked.

"One of them was named Beth," Will answered. "That's all you need to know."

Dave shook his head. "Beth's boyfriend was probably a bodybuilder," he said.

"That's never stopped him before," Zack replied with a grin. The laugher returned, all tension from hours before long forgotten. Hovering in the sky, the full moon cast a pale light across Drifter's Folly.

None of them noticed the figure watching them from the shadows.

CHAPTER FIVE

A QUIET WIND SWEPT THROUGH THE trees, causing leaves to cascade down to earth. Drifter's Folly Memorial Park was perfectly still. Not a trace of life stirred under the light of the full moon. Even the animals were hidden from view, as if they knew the hunt was coming.

The single tent at the peak of Whispering Reach lay silent under the specter of the pines. A smoldering heap of embers was all that remained of the campfire. The tent's occupants were sleeping. They wouldn't remain so much longer.

A man emerged from the darkness of the forest, wearing pistols and blades holstered underneath his jacket. There was a bow strapped to his back. The man's face was obscured by a black bandana tied around the lower half of his face, concealing his features. A pair of brown leather gloves covered his hands. The darkness did the rest.

Most of the park was visible from the apex of the cliff. He studied every inch of Drifter's Folly. There was nowhere they could hide—any of them. The others beyond Whispering Reach would hear his signal, and they too would run. Running might give them a few extra hours of life at most, but the same end was inevitable for all.

Black eyes gazed at the tent with hungry intent. The eyes flickered up to the moon. This was where Crowe cut out the animal's heart. This was where the hunt would begin. He turned and moved slowly toward the tent.

***

Zack was lying motionless in his sleeping bag when he heard the sound. For a moment, he felt Lily's presence in the tent. Zack looked around, half expecting to see her there.

She's dead, he thought finally. *She's never coming back.* Nothing could change that.

He rubbed his eyes and pulled the blankets higher, hoping to find rest. Despite the day's labors, sleep proved elusive. The others drifted off almost immediately after retiring to the tent. Cole was out like a light. Zack envied them. He listened for the sound again, wondering if it came from an animal. Aside from Dave's snores, he couldn't hear a thing. He closed his eyes and sighed.

He heard it again. Zack sat up. It was difficult to see anything outside the thin lining of the tent. Although the moon was shining brightly, everything was draped in shade. There was no sign of movement. He was about to lie back down when the sound echoed a third time.

Something was outside the tent.

"Is someone there?"

Will stirred at his feet. "What's going on?" he asked sleepily.

Zack didn't answer. A shadow appeared in front of the tent. As the form drew nearer, it took on the shape of a man.

Zack slid out of the sleeping bag. "Fields, is that you?"

Other than the sound of what sounded like boots scraping against the rocks somewhere outside the tent, there was no response.

"Go back to sleep," Will muttered. "It's just the wind." He closed his eyes, probably expecting Zack to do the same thing.

Zack couldn't. There were chill bumps on his arms. His hair stood on end. Something was wrong, and he knew it. Once before he experienced the same feeling of foreboding. He was closing down the bakery for the night when an overwhelming desire to call Lily gripped him. Zack ignored the feeling. The next day, he learned that a neighbor found Lily's body in her garage. She left her car running and let herself drift away.

He sank to his knees when he heard the news. Whatever it was, God or survivor's instinct, something had reached out to him, and he ignored the feeling. He wouldn't ignore it this time.

"Guys," he whispered forcefully, "wake up." He grabbed Cole and shook him.

"Just let me sleep a few more minutes," Cole mumbled, trying to pull away. Zack started unzipping the rear of the tent. The shadow expanded in size as the sound grew louder. Now Steve was awake.

"Stop it," Will said in a growl. "I told you it was nothing." He grabbed one of the two-way radios. "I'll prove it," he said. "Fields, are you there?"

There was no answer. Only static.

Before Zack could respond, a hand pulled down the zipper from outside the tent. Moonlight poured inside the tent, blinding the campers. Will froze.

"Fields?" Zack asked.

Underneath the mask of his bandana, the killer grinned. "Not quite."

Zack found his footing. His nerves were on fire. "Who the hell are you?" he demanded loudly.

The shape moved with alarming speed. He seized Zack by the shoulder and held a blade against his throat without cutting him.

"I'm someone who wants to play a little game," the killer answered.

Alarmed, Will climbed to his feet.

"Don't come any closer," the Hunter said harshly, "or I'll carve his face off."

Zack stood rooted to the spot, unable to speak. The killer seemed to stare into his very soul with eyes full of hate. The eyes burned black as coal, and there was no mistaking the evil intent. He was searching for something—a sign of weakness.

Don't show fear, a voice said inside Zack's head.

His impulse was to shake. Somehow he steeled his nerves and remained motionless. Still holding the knife, the killer turned his attention to the others.

"What do you want?" Will asked, looking around. Zack could tell what he was thinking. Whoever the intruder was, it was just one man with a knife. There were four of them inside the large tent, minus Zack. If they rushed the attacker they should be able to overwhelm him. He could see Will waiting for an opening. The others remained too sluggish to comprehend what was happening. They were starting to wake up. Cole stood behind him, followed by Steve. Dave was on his knees.

"You're asking the wrong question," the Hunter said. "How much do you want to live?" No one answered. "This is what will happen. You'll run, and death will come for you. As it comes for everything."

"You're insane," Will said.

The killer removed the blade from Zack's throat and held it inches from his right eye. It took all of Zack's willpower not to collapse. He bit his tongue and tasted blood.

"If any of you make it beyond the boundaries of the park, you won't be pursued. If you can last until first light, you will be spared."

The five campers looked at him incredulously. Only one of the men appeared to recognize the sincerity of the threat. When Zack saw the killer's gaze shift from Will to Steve, he realized something bad was about to happen. Steve was visibly trembling, on the verge of tears. Dave inched backwards toward the rear of the tent.

"Remember my words," the killer said. "Wherever you go, wherever you hide, I'll be watching. All of you." He slid the knife back into its holster and turned his back as if to go.

"Let's get out of here," Zack whispered to Will. He gestured toward the rear of the tent.

Before the others could react, the Hunter turned back around. This time, he was holding a gun.

He shot Steve through the chest. The roar of the gunshot shattered the stillness of the night, echoing for miles.

Dave was already sliding under the opening at the rear of the tent when Steve's body crumpled to the ground. Will and Cole followed mere seconds after as the campers tore out of the tent. Zack tumbled backwards, landing on his backside. The killer shifted the gun in his direction. Zack rolled out the back seconds before the masked man pulled the trigger.

"Run!" Cole shouted, casting a glance back at him.

Dave was already out of sight. Zack pushed himself off the ground. The killer was blocking the trail leading back to the lodge. There wasn't time to think. Zack scrambled after the others in the direction of Dead Man's Drop.

Dark clouds passed over the moon, concealing the night in a vast blackness. The narrow path down the cliff was perilous. Zack could hardly see two feet in front of him.

"Cole?" he shouted as he searched frantically for the others.

Zack didn't see the rock jutting out ahead of him until it was too late. He tripped and fell, sliding down the cliff. His pants ripped. He managed to catch himself before rolling off the side of Whispering Reach.

Dim light peeked out from behind the clouds. There was a small drop onto another ledge below. In the event he was still being pursued, it was unlikely the killer could follow him safely. He listened for the sound of his friends, but they were gone. Zack looked behind him. He couldn't see Steve's killer, but didn't mean the man wasn't there.

He had a choice to make. He could crawl back up and run down the side of the cliff exposed, or drop down and risk being separated from the others. Above, Zack thought he heard movement. Moving slowly so as not to fall again, he eased his way down the ledge. Praying he wasn't making a grievous error, he released his grip and fell until his feet connected with the rocky ledge. Zack followed the path for several minutes. He couldn't see far enough to be sure, but the rocky hill he was standing on led onto an unfamiliar forest trail.

Despite the temptation to call out for the others, Zack knew he was on his own for the time being. A cry for help would risk giving away his location. That was a risk he was unwilling to take.

What do I do now? he thought. The moon reemerged above, illuminating the path forward. Zack reluctantly started down the trail. There was no other way.

I'm on the wrong side of the lake, he realized. *We didn't come this way earlier.* He was lost and alone in Drifter's Folly. Somewhere out there, the man with the knife waited. Zack glanced up at the curved peak of Whispering Reach before fleeing toward the tentative safety of the forest. There was nothing there.

***

The entrance to the tent was abandoned. Steve was alone. The dying man inched forward. The bullet had passed through his chest just above his heart, shattering bone. It made little difference that his heart had been spared. Without medical care, he would be dead within minutes.

"Help," Steve croaked weakly. He clawed his way outside the tent, leaving a trail of blood in his wake. His vision swam, and he battled the urge to close his eyes. The blackness threatened to consume him.

He spilled out from the tent onto the rocky earth. Steve tried to cry out again, but no sound escaped his lips. Where were the others? It took a while for the crushing realization to set in. They thought he was dead. He'd been left behind.

He heard a sound in the dark.

"Guys?" he whispered.

The figure standing under the trees wasn't one of his friends.

Steve's face whitened with terror. The killer was waiting for him all along.

"No," he tried to protest as the killer grabbed him by his feet, dragging him along the cliff.

The killer knelt at his side. The man's black eyes gleamed in the moonlight. He removed the knife he used to threaten Zack. Steve's heart thundered in panic. Just before the killer buried the blade into his chest, Steve thought he saw something shiny hanging from the man's neck. His voice didn't travel past the cliff. No one could hear him screaming.

***

When the killer completed the ritual, he threw the corpse down from the cliff. He waited for the body to hit the water below. The Hunter watched until the dead man vanished into Dire Lake. His gaze shifted to the forest, and he scanned the valley for the others.

He saw no trace of movement. Perhaps the campers would make it challenging for him after all.

"It has begun," he said. He clutched his necklace tightly. The wind roared around him, carrying the echoes of whispers. The first death was meaningless. It served only as a trigger, to get the wheels in motion. The true hunt was just getting started.

Leaving Whispering Reach behind, the killer retreated to Beggar's Road. From there he entered a hidden path. The hunting bow and arrows were waiting under the tree where he left them. He delved into a sack and removed a pair of night-vision goggles. The killer switched the goggles on.

The four men camped on Whispering Reach were only part of the game. There were more campers across the park. Drifter's Folly was the perfect hunting ground. The others across the valley would have heard the gunshot. Cell phones were of no use. They would try to radio in and find no response, and then they would run or hide. Either way, he would find them.

He always did.

CHAPTER SIX

THE SPECTER OF DIRE LAKE loomed through the trees. The vast body of water glowed under the moonlight. Three men tore into the forest, shattering the silence of the night. Will felt the others begin to slow behind him. He cast a quick glance in every direction to see if they were being followed. It was impossible to tell.

"We don't have time to stop," he said. "We have to keep going." The trail leading from Whispering Reach was less than sixty yards behind them.

Dave shook his head and sank to the ground. The heavy man vomited, a retching sound that disgusted Will. Cole was leaning against a tree, panting. Zack was gone. Will swore. He wished he were still dreaming, lying inside the tent. Instead, he was living a waking nightmare.

Cole stared in the direction of Dead Man's Drop, as if waiting for Zack. Sweat trickled down to his glasses. The law student had removed his contact lenses before bed and was now stuck wearing a pair of old reading glasses.

"He's not coming," Will said, unsure if he was referring to Zack or the maniac from the tent.

He watched as Cole felt around in the pocket of his pants for his cell phone. To Will's surprise, his friend pulled out the phone.

Of all the people in the tent, he was the only one who always kept his phone with him. Will hoped against hope for a signal as Cole turned on the phone.

"No signal," Cole muttered bitterly. "Ranger Fields wasn't kidding."

It took Will several moments before realizing he was still clutching the two-way radio in his hand. He pressed the call button, hoping to get a response from Fields.

"Hello?" Like before, there was only static on the other end. Will switched to another channel and tried again. "Is anyone there?"

Nothing. His fist tightened around the small device. His jaw clenched in anger. Will wanted to toss the thing into the lake, but thought better of it. He slid the walkie-talkie into his pocket for safekeeping.

"What are we going to do?" Dave moaned loudly, his palms pressed against the grass.

Leaves rustled in the woods behind them. Will held a finger to his mouth, motioning for Dave to shut up. The thing in the forest drew nearer. The three men tensed, expecting the worst.

A deer stepped into a clearing in front of them. The animal picked at the ground beneath its hooves, oblivious to their presence. The wind shifted in the opposite direction, and the deer looked up at them before bounding away toward the lake.

Will sighed in relief. He grabbed Dave by the arm and pulled him up.

"Keep your voices down," he whispered. "Anyone could be listening." He looked back at Cole. "We need to move."

Cole wiped his glasses with his t-shirt and shook his head. "Not without Zack."

"Your friend's not coming back," Dave muttered. His eyes were focused not on Cole, but the cliff just beyond the trees. "He's dead, just like Steve."

"We don't know that," Cole said. He looked to Will for support.

"I'm with Dave on this," Will said reluctantly. "Maybe Zack got away. Maybe he didn't. We don't know. Staying here and waiting for someone to come along will only get us killed." He started forward and motioned for them to follow. "Come on."

The others didn't budge.

"Where are we going?" Dave asked.

"To find someplace to hide. He's just one man. He can't be everywhere."

"We need to get help," Cole said. "There are other people in the park."

"There's nothing we can do for them," Will replied. "In case you haven't noticed, the radio Fields gave us isn't even working. We need to look out for ourselves first."

Dave nodded. The two men walked farther into the forest. Cole scanned the trail for Zack one last time before following. They walked in silence for several minutes, stopping several times and crouching behind trees when anyone heard a noise. Each time they waited for something that never emerged.

"Do we even know where we're going?" Dave whispered.

"We're close to Shatter Creek Trail," Will replied.

It was quickly becoming obvious the other two would be lost without him. They hadn't spent long in the forest earlier, but Will thought he knew the lay of the land well enough to get around. If they lost their way, it would spell disaster. He suspected the killer knew the ins and outs of Drifter's Folly well. If Fields was right, the man had been stalking the trails for weeks. He thought of Zack. If his friend was out there, he was best equipped to survive on his own. Cole was an inexperienced camper, and Dave's experience was virtually nonexistent.

"Why go that way?" Dave said. "The creek is visible from the cliff."

"We'll risk it," Will replied. Having walked it before during the day, he was most familiar with that particular trail. Besides, it was close to the river.

"I think we should go back," Dave said.

"Toward the killer?" Cole whispered.

"We're going farther into the park. We should be trying to get away. Our van is back at the lodge."

Will had taken the keys from Zack after they parked the van. He frowned and inched his hand into his right pocket. His expression fell when he found empty space.

"The keys are in the tent," he said. He'd left them behind.

"Maybe we could find other keys in the lodge," Dave volunteered, "or try to make it to the highway."

Will grabbed Dave's shoulders. "We're not going back," he said forcefully. "The killer is that way, so we're going the opposite direction."

"What if there's a phone in the lodge?" Dave asked. "We could call for help." He searched for Cole's eyes in the dark. "Maybe your cell phone will work at the lodge."

"A phone," Cole muttered.

Will thought he saw recognition on his friend's face. "What is it?" he asked.

"You said we're close to Shatter Creek Trail. Remember the payphone we saw at the recreation center? We can call for help."

Will might have hugged him. "Anyone have any change?" To his surprise, Dave nodded.

"I always carry my wallet with me." Dave was still wearing his blue jeans.

"Let's go," Will said.

It didn't take long to find the trail that led to the recreation area. The three men followed the path of the creek, listening to the sounds coming from the woods. Cole and Dave continued to lag behind Will. The afternoon hike was already starting to catch up with Dave. Cole was wearing only socks. Running down Dead

Man's Drop hadn't done him any favors. Will couldn't tell in the dim light, but it looked like his socks were already streaked with blood. He considered himself lucky he was wearing shoes. They were on a dirt trail now, so Cole was okay for the moment. Will didn't want to think about what would happen if they were forced to continue their walk indefinitely. He swore he wouldn't let his friend slow them down, if it came to that.

When they reached a part of the trail he didn't remember, Will stopped and tried to figure out which way to go. Everything looked different in the dark. None of his experience prepared him for this. Cole was watching him expectantly, and Will wasn't about to admit he was lost. The last thing he needed was for either of the others to panic. Dave looked like he was barely hanging on as it was.

"I think we're close," he said, hoping he was right. Will was about to start again when something caught his eye. "Stop," he said to Dave. He held a hand in front of the man's chest.

"What is it?" Cole asked.

"Get down," Will whispered. The three men crouched and stared down the trail. A few seconds later, Will pointed at something ahead. "See that?"

Cole squinted through his glasses. The prescription on the old pair was long out of date. "I don't see anything."

"Neither do I," Dave whispered.

"It's a trip wire," Will said. He crept closer. He didn't want to know what would happen if they tripped it.

"A what?"

"It's part of a trap."

He felt the ground with his hand until he found a large rock. Will hurled the stone at the wire and jumped back. For a moment nothing happened. Then a swishing sound echoed above them as a spear swung from the tree just outside the shore of the river. The sharpened log smashed into a second tree on the other side of the trail, tearing through bark. The three men walked over to the log, which was hanging from a thick rope tied to one end.

Cole ran his hand along the spear, stopping at its jagged end. "That would have been us."

"What does it mean?" Dave asked.

Will thought about it for a moment. For some reason, the spear reminded him of the bear trap Zack spotted when he and Cole were near the cave. The image clicked with the words the killer said inside their tent.

"This isn't just some lunatic with a gun. He's *hunting us*."

Dave shook his head. "There has to be some other explanation."

"There isn't. How do you explain the bear trap you found? He's been planning this for weeks. There are probably other traps hidden around the park." Even as he spoke the words, Will didn't want to believe them. Unfortunately, he couldn't afford the luxury of denial. "We need to be careful," he said. "Let's get off the trail."

The others followed Will as he headed in what he thought was the direction of the recreation area. Each moment felt like an hour. He kept expecting something to jump out at him from the darkness. The not knowing was worst of all. Will wondered if that was what the killer wanted them to feel.

He was about to go farther into the forest when Dave tugged on his arm.

"We're here," he whispered.

Will turned and peered through the bushes. The outline of the volleyball court was just visible in the shadowy recesses of the forest. The three men carefully made their way up to the bushes. A dim yellow light glowed from the solitary light pole behind the table area. Rather than making the area seem safer, the flickering light made the region stand out from the dark night, and not in a good way.

The recreation area was abandoned. There was no sign of life anywhere around. The only noise came from the tire swing moving back and forth in the breeze. Abandoning any pretext of hiding, the three men ran out of the forest toward the payphone. Dave scrambled through his pockets for change and slid a quarter into the slot. Will's pulse raced. Everyone was staring at the phone. Dave held it up to his ear.

"There's nothing there," he said. His voice broke.

Will took the phone from his hand and listened. There was no dial tone, no nothing. The phone was out of order.

***

Cole sank to the ground against the light pole. He caressed his throbbing feet, which ached all the more with the realization they would soon be walking again. Dave stumbled over to the tables and sat down. Will remained standing with the phone in his hand, staring into the distance. Pale moonlight was reflected off the water, illuminating the area beyond the forest. The three men didn't move for several moments. Each contemplated the magnitude of their shared misfortune.

Cole was struck by the change moonlight brought to the scenery around them. The recreation area, with its faded lettering and lack of repairs, was at best unsettling during the day. Under the moon, it was beyond frightening. He wasn't sure if the thoughts occurred naturally, or if everything had taken a darker tone now that they were being pursued. He wasn't sure he cared.

It was Will who spoke first.

"We can't stay here," he said, turning to face the others. "We should move on."

Cole pushed up his glasses. "We need to rest and sort this out," he said. "Running scared and blind is what we don't need to do."

Dave rose from the table. When he spoke, the agitation in his voice was clear. "Do you remember what I said earlier about the lodge? That's where we should go."

Will's opinion remained unchanged. "I told you, that's the

wrong direction to go. No matter how well the killer knows the forest, this park is way too large for him to find us if we stay ahead of him until sunrise."

"You're assuming he'll keep his word," Cole said. "What if sunrise comes and he's still out there waiting for us to come out?"

"It doesn't matter," Will said. "If we keep going, we'll reach the end of the park eventually. It may take days, but we'll get out of this." Unspoken was the impact the lack of food and water would have on such an endeavor.

After considering the matter, Cole finally agreed. "That may be our best bet. We can stop to rest and try to contact Fields every hour or so." Cole stared down at his feet. He would probably need to rest more frequently than that.

"How can you agree with him?" Dave asked Cole. He turned from Will and stood in front of him, looking down on Cole. "He just said there were probably tons of traps waiting for us out there. If we go farther into the park we run the risk of getting totally lost." He glanced back at Will. "Let's face it, there's no way we'll find the end of the park. We'll end up walking in circles for days. Once the sun rises, we'll be sitting ducks."

Dave's words were coherent, but his voice sounded like he was coming apart. He was starting to rant, waving his hands in the air and making animated gestures. Cole didn't like that Dave's voice was growing louder.

"You're both forgetting about Ranger Fields and Hickory Johnson. Eventually someone is going to discover something is wrong. The killer can't stay here forever unless he wants to get caught. It's just a matter of time," Cole said. "Don't forget, it isn't like we can drive away. The car keys are inside the tent."

"It's settled then," Will said. "We're not going back."

"It's *not* settled," Dave said emphatically. He pointed at Cole. "You still have your cell phone. Let's try and find a spot where you can get in range."

A cloud passed over the moon again, dimming the sky.

"I don't want to waste my battery," Cole replied. "We need to be careful with what we have." The wind stopped. Will looked around, suspicion in his eyes. "What's wrong?" Cole asked.

"I thought I heard something," Will muttered. Despite his calm demeanor, he seemed unusually jumpy.

Out of nowhere, an object sailed out of the darkness and hit the flickering light. The light shattered, glass spilling down on Cole. Dave jumped back.

Without the light, the recreation area was covered in the shadows of the forest. Cole's eyes locked on the projectile. It was an arrow with a razor sharp tip. He looked up at Will, his eyes widening in terror. Will was standing in the open, with nothing behind him except the water. He dropped down, looking everywhere for the direction the arrow came from. The killer was there somewhere, but where?

Cole hurled himself under the tables. He prayed the killer couldn't see them in the darkness. Dave stood against a tree, separated from the other two by several open feet. As he started to move in their direction, a second arrow lodged itself in the tree, inches from him.

He's got us pinned down, Cole thought. His mind raced. *How did he find us so quickly?* From underneath the tables, Cole pointed in the direction of the forest. Will shook his head, as if to imply they couldn't go back into the woods without knowing if the killer was right behind them. Each second they waited was agonizing. No matter how hard he looked, he couldn't even catch a glimpse of the killer's location. It was like the man was invisible.

Suddenly, Will flung himself into the open and ran toward the woods, leaving the others behind. Cole scrambled to get free from under the tables and raced across the volleyball court. He kicked up sand underneath his feet as he went. No arrows followed either man.

"Come on!" Cole shouted to Dave from the safety of the

bushes. Dave stood rooted to the tree trunk, breathing heavily. He was panicking. "Dave, we have to go!" Cole's voice shook Dave from his trance. The large man stepped into the moonlight and ran toward the woods.

Right when he neared the edge of the forest, a third arrow flew straight for him.

"Look out!" Cole shouted. He was too late. Dave moved, but not quite enough to get out of the way. The arrow tore through the side of his shirt and careened into the darkness. Dave screamed and fell forward just a few feet shy of the cover of the forest.

"Dave!" Cole yelled, moving to help. Completely exposed, Dave was a sitting duck.

Will grabbed his arm. "Leave him!"

Cole broke free of Will's grasp and jumped through the bushes. He seized Dave by the wrist and pulled him up. Two more arrows passed by seconds after they entered the forest.

The three men ran as fast as they could in no direction in particular. Hell was chasing them, and there was no refuge to be found.

CHAPTER SEVEN

11:44 PM

IN THE WEEKS FOLLOWING LILY's confession, life lost all meaning for him. Baking became a chore rather than a hobby. Zack found himself too unfocused for reading, which had always proven his favorite form of escapism. He went to church with Cole a few times, though he was really just walking through the motions. In the end, his friends were his saving grace. Will was determined that he have a good time, and his enthusiasm eventually rubbed off on Zack. For a while, he almost forgot about Lily and her betrayal, but something in the back of his mind never quite let him forget entirely.

When Lily took her life, all the feelings came rushing back. Only this time, he couldn't blame her. Unlike his previous battle with melancholy, he distanced himself from his friends. He couldn't bother with anyone else, not when each day was a struggle to get by. Though he tried to fight it, Zack had never stopped loving Lily. He knew he could never allow himself to get back together with her, but he regretted cutting her out of his life completely.

He became obsessed with discovering the identity of the person she'd been seeing, something he never cared about before. The stranger was someone else he could blame. Zack tried tracking down Lily's friends for more information, only to find she really didn't have any. Talking to her family was almost impossible. A coworker mentioned Lily crying shortly after their breakup about feeling used. From what Zack could piece together, the mystery man probably wasn't someone she'd actually had a prolonged relationship with. Maybe Lily was looking for something more, only she never got it. Zack wondered if this was what she was seeking help for when she called him.

He never found the solace he was seeking, and it was likely he never would. As he found himself standing in the heart of Drifter's Folly, Zack knew he was lost in more ways than one. He looked around, searching for some element of his surroundings he might have glimpsed earlier in the day. There was nothing familiar, not that it mattered in the dark. He hoped the others had flashlights or something else to guide them. He was too deep in the forest for the moonlight to be much help.

While being lost frightened him, it also gave him the opportunity to regain his bearings. Zack searched for a weapon. The killer certainly possessed one. The memory of the blade held against his throat testified to that.

He's coming for you, said a voice inside his head. *Why bother resisting at all? Maybe giving up is the best thing.* Zack held no answer for the doubts. They were the same that plagued him after Lily's death.

Sometimes he wondered why he even bothered going on. If life held no meaning, was it worth living? Something in him kept going on, some spark of life. It was the shadow of a hope. Zack didn't know what there was left to hope in, but it was something to hold onto all the same.

"You're a survivor," Lily's mother had said. She was right. The killer might find him anyway, but Zack didn't intend to make it easy for him.

The wind howled loudly above. Zack could hardly feel the breeze inside the dense forest. He wondered if the others were also lost. Cole was the last person he saw before falling in the darkness.

If they made it down Dead Man's Drop, they might have a chance of outpacing the killer until sunrise—unless they too were scattered, separated on the myriad of trails across Drifter's Folly.

After several minutes of aimless wandering, Zack spotted a beam of light pouring across the trees. Hesitantly musing which course to take, he made his way up a small slope toward the light. Zack found himself standing in a grassy field in what appeared to be the middle of nowhere. The moon was shining brightly above the grove, which was surrounded on all sides by forest. A small log building rested almost seventy yards away, covered in the moonlight.

Where am I? As Zack waded through the tall weeds, he tried to remember all the sites listed on the map. The tiny wooden structure was too small to be one of the cabins they passed on the way to Whispering Reach. It was little more than a shed.

The wind died down suddenly, and his footsteps echoed in the darkness. Although he knew no one could hear him unless they were close, the noise still gave him chills. Before he reached the shed, Zack's foot slid over something hard. He tripped and landed outside the weeds in a small pasture behind the building. Zack rose and dusted himself off. When his eyes adjusted to the light, he realized he wasn't standing in a pasture at all. He was standing in a graveyard.

For a moment he couldn't breathe. The cemetery was surrounded on three sides by spiky black fence. A rusted gate hung open beside the shed, covered in overgrowth. From the look of things, the graveyard had been left untended for some time. Zack stood in place, his eyes flickering from tombstone to tombstone. Most of the graves were small or broken. Letters and names were long since faded, and on some stones there were no markings at all. All the tombstones were either a dirty gray or a dark black.

What was a cemetery doing in the park? He didn't know, but the graveyard's mere presence was disturbing. The cemetery was impossibly large considering the size of the grove. Graves stretched in every direction. Zack didn't know when Drifter's Folly was designated a state park, but it was likely the graves predated the park's existence. He forced himself to remember that a killer of flesh and blood, not a spectral predator, was pursuing him. The realization did little to calm his nerves.

An owl watched him from a tree next to the shed. Zack found the eerie gaze unsettling. A faint sound echoed in the distance, and Zack quickly looked up. He searched around the forest looming not far away, peering through the blackness for forces unseen.

"Guys?" he asked, his voice barely above a whisper. "Will?" he asked again, louder.

There was nothing there. He was alone. Considering his present straights, that was either a good thing or a very bad thing.

Keenly aware of his exposure in the open field, he walked toward the gate. A metal plaque with gold lettering greeted him on the way out of the cemetery. The words glowed under the moonlight. They read, *Drifter's Folly Graveyard*. Zack let the words sink in as he neared the shed. The diminutive building was larger than it appeared against the backdrop of the field. The wooden planks comprising the hut's exterior were splintered and worn. There was a sign on a small post a few inches from the shed's front door. *Park Museum,* read the plank.

Zack read it again. It was impossible to believe the shed was the park's so-called museum. Even hikers purposefully looking for the landmark would have difficulty finding it. There were no trails around the grove as far as he could see. *Maybe there's a phone inside,* Zack thought, *or a computer.* Both possibilities struck him as unlikely at best. He eased the door handle open and stepped inside. The door creaked unevenly on rusted hinges as it swung shut behind him.

Moonlight streamed through foggy windows on two sides of the building. Even with the pale beams of light, the hut was incredibly dark. Zack took a few steps forward and bumped into a desk. He felt around for a light and flipped the switch. Nothing happened. Zack swore silently before spotting an old yellow flashlight lying on the desk. To his surprise, it worked.

Zack pointed the beam straight in front of him. There were two to three plaques on each of the four walls, all containing information about the park. Several large black-and-white pictures also hung from the walls. Antique relics were cased under glass containers, several of which were covered in cobwebs. Chairs and desks were pushed or stacked against the walls as well. He guessed the museum hadn't been in use for a while.

Aside from the dust, the one-room building was remarkably well preserved. He shone the beam around the hut, searching for a phone. No such luck. Between the cemetery and the shed, it was like he had stepped into the nineteenth century. One of the photos on the wall caught his eye. The picture depicted the graveyard many years earlier, when the grove was clear of weeds. A small band of mourners were gathered in the cemetery, listening to a preacher. Wagons and horses were barely visible near the edges of the picture.

Zack read the caption. *Drifter's Folly, as the territory became known, began along a trading route bridging two settlements. Bandits or natives frequently attacked traders and travelers alike. This led to the territory's name, which served as a warning to anyone wandering through the forest.*

He turned to another picture, one showing a military regiment assembled on Whispering Reach. *A squadron of soldiers from Fort Perseverance gathered here following the Battle of Fallen Weeds. The soldiers engaged an unknown Native American tribe, resulting in massive casualties on both sides.*

Zack wondered how many of the combatants were buried in the cemetery. He remembered what Fields said about the serial killer. Zack wondered if the park's history was the reason the Hunter picked Drifter's Folly for his latest murder spree.

After taking a few steps back, Zack searched the hut for

anything else that might prove helpful. His footsteps tracked dusty prints across the dirty floor. A large spider scurried beneath him, vanishing into a cranny in the wall. Zack looked up and found a map displaying the landmarks and trails of the park. Shining the light at the map, he traced the paths with his fingers. He tried to commit the sight to memory, like he should have done from the beginning.

His nerves were the definition of frayed. He felt safe in the abandoned shed, but it was impossible to be sure how long he could remain there. Outside, the wind began howling again. Or was it something else? Zack walked over to one of the cloudy windowpanes. He rubbed the glass with the flat of his palm, forming a small window. As far as he could see, there was nothing outside the shed. He was about to turn around when his eyes saw a gleam in the darkness.

That was when Zack saw him. A dark figure was standing at the end of the forest beyond the cemetery. Moonlight glimmered off the barrel of the man's gun. The figure was staring straight at him. Zack's hair stood on end. He immediately switched the flashlight off and dropped out of sight. Zack sank against the wall below the window and sat silently in the darkness of the shed. The flashlight hung lifelessly from his hand.

How did he find me? The figure was standing too far away to be certain it was the same deranged individual who entered their tent. Zack was certain it wasn't one of his friends. Whoever it was, the man had a gun. That alone made him dangerous.

Zack waited a few moments, his mind racing furiously as he tried to think of a way to escape. Each route proved perilous or unknown. There was enough distance between him and the man with the gun that Zack could probably escape into the forest the way he came. That path would end in Whispering Reach, and he would be cornered.

Gathering his courage, he rose and stared out the window again to catch a glimpse of the figure. The man was gone. Zack scanned the darkness, desperately searching for the man who was watching him mere seconds ago. His heart raced. Zack scrambled to his feet and headed for the door. If he didn't act now, the figure might reach him within minutes. With luck, he could slip outside the museum and disappear into the field.

He held the flashlight in one hand and eased the door open. The door creaked even louder than before. Moonlight washed over him as he stepped outside, temporarily overwhelming his sense of sight. Zack took several steps in the direction of the cemetery. Suddenly, a group of tall weeds near the hut started to shift. Footsteps echoed in the night. Zack ran back through the graveyard, fighting against the wind. He cast a brief glance behind him as he cleared the fence. The man with the shotgun was now standing next to the shed. Mustering all his energy, Zack ignored the lactic acid building up in his legs and kept going. He could feel the man's gaze following him. The figure started after him. Although the man was moving fast, Zack was nearly to the edge of the forest.

"Wait!" he thought he heard the figure shout, but Zack was already too far away to tell for sure.

He left the grove behind and entered the forest. His foot tripped over a rock and he barely had time to correct himself from falling. The darkness forced him to slow his pace, but he continued moving as quickly as he could afford. While he could no longer see his pursuer, Zack sensed he was still being followed.

I need to find a trail, he thought as he stumbled through the forest. He tried to remember the paths displayed on the map. Zack wished he'd spent more attention studying the rendering earlier when he had the chance. Recalling his therapy sessions, he tried not to blame himself. None of them could have expected this.

A voice rang out again, and it was loud and clear.

"Where are you?" his pursuer called.

He couldn't see the man anywhere. Zack guessed he had

managed to put a good deal of distance between himself and the figure. He kept going until he no longer heard the sound of rustling leaves behind him. The scenery changed, and he thought he heard the river roaring in the distance.

If I find the river, I'll find the trails. With luck, it would also lead him to the others. *If I know Will, he'll be following the water.*

When he was confident he was no longer being followed, he slowed to a quiet walk. The shadows might work to the killer's advantage, but they could work to conceal Zack as well. His heartbeat eventually returned to a steady rhythm, though he was still breathing heavily. His clothes were drenched in sweat. At least his leg no longer hurt from the fall down Dead Man's Drop.

He made his way across a winding creek. Based on the proximity of the creek to the museum, Zack guessed the flowing water was either Snowfall Creek or Shatter Creek. Snowfall Creek trickled down from the mountains, while Shatter Creek merged with the river flowing into Dire Lake. He paused, unsure of what to do. Before he could make up his mind, an echo rang through the forest. People were shouting behind him to the east, in the direction following the creek.

Zack wanted to holler, but he didn't want to give away his position in the unlikely scenario he was still being followed. Instead, he ran in the direction of the shouts, hoping he wasn't making a mistake. He might find his friends. He realized that if they were under attack, finding them might not be a good thing. On the other hand, there seemed to be no way Zack's pursuer could have outpaced him and reached his friends. It didn't make sense.

"Come on!" one of the voices shouted.

That sounded like Cole, Zack thought. He was close. Zack peered through the dense layer of trees, trying to locate the source of the sound. He could see nothing in the forest other than blackness and moonlight. As he ran, he passed a narrow dirt trail. Zack turned onto the trail. The shouts were becoming faint. He was losing them.

The dirt path led him into a small clearing away from the creek. Zack looked in every direction, no longer certain where he was going. He stepped off the path, and his right foot met resistance as it passed over the earth. When he looked down, he saw a black wire shining under the moonlight. Before Zack could react, something wrapped around his foot. He was swiftly pulled into the air by a rope suspended from one of the tree branches. The rope swung quickly, and Zack saw the massive tree truck seconds before his face smashed into it.

The last thing he heard were footsteps approaching the clearing. Then everything went black.

CHAPTER EIGHT

ZACK AWOKE WITH A START. His head throbbed and his vision swam. As he stared down, he could feel blood rushing to his head. He was hanging upside-down facing a tree, a full body length off the ground.

How long was I out? Zack tried to regain his bearings. It didn't feel like he was unconscious for long, though it was impossible to tell.

As his head cleared, he became vaguely aware of a presence nearby. For a moment, he thought he could see Lily's face watching him from below. The image sharpened, and he realized it wasn't Lily after all. Instead, it was a blonde woman he'd never met. Standing next to a bulky man wearing a frown, the woman watched him with suspicion.

"He's awake," the man said.

Now that he could see clearly, Zack realized the woman barely resembled Lily. Her hair was lighter than Lily's, and her face and figure were fuller. Lily was rail thin while they dated, probably stemming from her fast-paced lifestyle and frantic energy. It was only on the occasions when she was depressed that she ate anything other than fruits or vegetables.

Zack tugged at the rope binding his foot in an effort to free himself. "If you aren't here to kill me," he said to the couple, "I could use some help."

The pair exchanged glances. Finally, the woman nodded. "I

think we should get him down from there," she whispered nervously to her companion.

"Are you sure?" the man asked, also in a hushed voice.

Zack could hear everything they said. After a few seconds, the man approached the tree and took out a sharp knife. The man slowly cut through the rope until Zack felt himself fall. He hit the soft earth with a thud.

"Don't move," the man said, holding the knife close to Zack's throat. He then patted him down for weapons. For the moment, Zack was glad he was unarmed. The knife shone brightly under the moonlight. Zack eyed the blade carefully. Only a few hours ago another knife had been held against his throat. He wasn't enthused about the prospect of it happening again.

"If you try anything," the man said, "I won't hesitate to use this."

Choked up from the fall, he shook his head silently to convey to the stranger that he meant no harm. The man narrowed his eyes and took two steps back.

"Start talking," the man said. "Who are you?"

Zack rose and climbed to his feet. The sudden movement appeared to spook the woman. Her companion rested a reassuring hand on her shoulder. Even considering the circumstances, the touching gesture made Zack envious.

"My name is Zack Allen." Zack held up his hands as if to indicate he wasn't a threat. He remembered Will mentioning running into two campers near the recreation area. Was this the blonde woman he was talking about? "You might know my friends," he added quickly. "Will? Dave and Steve?"

"Those are the guys we met earlier in the park," the woman said to the man with the knife.

"The one who couldn't keep his eyes off you," her companion muttered.

The petty comment struck Zack as silly considering the

circumstances, until he remembered his own flashbacks to Lily and changed his mind. Latching onto the things that made them human in a crisis seemed only natural.

"I'm Ron," the man said, "and this is Beth." Ron returned the blade to his belt, but he kept a close eye on Zack.

"Thanks for cutting me down," Zack said warily. "I don't know what I would have done if you hadn't come along."

Ron nodded. "We were following the creek when we heard you."

"We're lost," Beth added.

Ron clenched his jaw. He looked as if he wished she hadn't said the words. "We're not lost," he corrected. "We just need to find the trail and we'll be able to start our way back."

"You're going back?" Zack asked. He shook his head. "There was someone behind me that way," he said, glancing over his shoulder.

Ron's expression darkened. "Who was following you?" he demanded, looking agitated. Although Ron was shorter than Zack by several inches, the man was far more muscular. Not to mention he had a knife. Zack didn't want to give him reason to use it.

"I don't know," Zack answered honestly. "He had a gun, but it could have been anyone. I wasn't going to stick around and find out."

"Where are your friends?" Ron asked suspiciously.

"We got separated on the way down the cliff."

"What happened?" Beth asked. "We were about to go to sleep a few hours ago when we heard more gunshots." There was fear in her eyes, and Zack couldn't blame her.

"We think they came from the cliff. That's where you were camping."

The memory of Steve's death flashed through Zack's mind. He could smell the Hunter's rancid breath on his face. The dead eyes under the black bandana haunted him. It all came rushing back.

"We were sleeping," Zack whispered. "I heard something

outside the tent. A man stepped inside and threatened us. He said he would hunt us until dawn. Then he shot one of my friends."

Ron's mouth dropped open. "Fields was right," the man muttered. He glanced at Beth, who appeared staggered by the news.

"We tried to radio Fields when we heard the shots. He didn't answer."

That stopped Zack cold. If Fields still wasn't answering, he was either gone for the night or dead. In either event, they were alone.

"This isn't happening," Beth whispered, shaking. "It can't."

"Calm down," Ron said. Perhaps it was because he was too was on edge, but Ron's words didn't come off particularly reassuring.

"I was looking for my friends when I came across this trap," Zack said, almost to himself. "There's no telling what else is waiting for us."

"We found two bear traps after we started walking," Beth volunteered. "After Fields' story, Ron didn't want to stay near the tent until we knew more."

"The man who was following you—the man who killed your friends—what did he look like?" Ron asked.

Zack could remember the image as if the killer was still staring him in the eyes.

"He was wearing dark clothes," Zack said slowly. "A black bandana covered his face. He had at least one gun and a hunting knife."

"What exactly did he tell you?"

"He said he would hunt us. If we could get out of the park or survive until dawn, he said he would let us go."

There was a pause as each person contemplated the situation. The wind whistled through the trees, mingling with the sound of the distant creek. After seeing his flashlight under the tree, Zack bent down and picked it up.

He was first to break the silence.

"We have to keep moving. We have to stay ahead of him."

"Three people would be easier to spot than two," Ron whispered.
Beth looked shocked. "We can't leave him by himself."

"I can help you navigate the park," Zack said. "I know the outdoors. No matter how skilled this person is, there's no way he can find everyone in a park this size. Together maybe we can find some help." He saw that Ron was wearing a watch. "What time is it?"

"It's a few minutes after midnight. We've got the whole night ahead of us."

"Then come on," Zack said. He led them away from the trees, where the light was brighter. "Let's go this way," he added. "I think we're close to Shatter Creek Trail."

The moonlight glowed around them. When Zack turned around, Beth's expression changed. She pointed at his chest.

"Oh my God." She held up her hand to her mouth.

It wasn't until that moment that Zack noticed his shirt was stained in Steve's blood.

As Beth screamed, Ron pulled his knife.

***

The three men plunged ever deeper into the forest, scrambling like blind animals. Will knew the others were depending on him to lead the way, but that no longer concerned him. He was only interesting in staying alive. Everything else was secondary.

Having left the creek behind at the recreation area, they were running toward regions unknown. Will's legs started to burn as the terrain shifted upward. Still he pressed forward. The sounds of the others grew faint.

Will stumbled and nearly lost his footing. He was standing on a ledge. Although the cliff was smaller than Whispering Reach, a drop from that height would probably be deadly. The river rushed below, encircling the cliff in a crescent moon. Will dropped to his knees and waited to catch his breath.

"There's nothing below," he said when Cole and Dave emerged from the brush. "We're cornered."

"Then we have to go back," Cole said. "We can find another trail." Will already started to rise and Cole grabbed his arm. "Wait. We need to take a look at Dave first."

Will shot a dark look at Cole. Couldn't he see they were being pursued? Any delay could prove fatal. Sighing, he joined his friend at Dave's side, where the heavy man rested against a tree.

"How do you feel?" Will asked. He knelt and looked at Dave's side. The wound was shallow, but he was losing blood. Dave's face was pale.

"I feel light-headed," Dave whispered, struggling to sit up straight.

"You're lucky you don't have two arrows in you," Cole said. "If you hadn't moved when you did, you'd be a dead man."

Dave stared into Cole's eyes, expressing silent thanks for helping him out of the killer's line of fire, and Cole nodded curtly.

"Hold still," Will said. He looked over the wound. If they didn't get medicine, Dave ran the risk of getting infected. At the moment, that was low on their list of priorities. There were bandages back at the lodge, though Will wasn't sure that was where they needed to go. "You'll be fine for now, big guy," he said. He patted Dave on the knee. It was a lie, though the other two seemed to buy it. While Dave's injury wasn't mortal, he needed to get off his feet and rest. Will couldn't allow that.

Cole grabbed his shoulder. "How did he find us?"

Will didn't know. "He must have been following us down the cliff. He probably killed Zack first."

Oddly, Will didn't recall being followed as they made the descent from Dead Man's Drop, but it was the only explanation. Otherwise, how could the Hunter have tracked them?

"He was toying with us. We were just lucky he wasn't using bullets. If he wanted to kill us, he could have."

It was a miracle they all survived. The second run-in with the killer convinced him of one thing—the man hadn't been lying to them about his intentions. He murdered Steve and probably Zack, and they were all next. Will wanted to find a way out quickly.

"Let's go back down," Cole suggested. "We can follow the river."

The idea was as good as any. Will waited for Cole to help Dave off the ground, and the three men made their way back down the cliff the way they came. They were walking considerably slower than earlier. Even Will was showing signs of fatigue. They couldn't keep going like this.

Surely he won't find us again, Will thought. The Hunter was only human. He had limits, no matter how skilled a tracker he might be. On the other hand, that was what Will thought before the killer somehow found them again at the recreation area.

"We'll take this path," Will said once they were at the bottom of the hill. It diverged from the trail they took to reach the cliff. Will didn't know where they were heading, but he couldn't help feeling they were simply trekking back in the direction of Beggar's Road. Maybe Dave's idea to go back to the lodge wasn't such a bad one after all.

The river roared in the background. They entered a valley whose name Will no longer recalled. If his memory served him, they were east of the cabins in the mountains and west of Whispering Reach and Dire Lake. The valley was flooded. Will's pants were already covered in mud. Several times he had to catch Cole before he slipped. It looked like Cole tried not to show it, but the lack of shoes was causing him trouble.

The land grew drier the farther they traveled, though it remained damp at best. The trees were taller, and the mountains loomed not far from where they were. Dry leaves coated the ground.

"Maybe we should hike to the cabins," Dave said. "We could barricade the doors and hide out until sunrise. They might have phones inside."

"Quiet," Will said as he tried to listen for noises above the sound of the river.

Dave's idea wasn't particularly appealing. While the mountains weren't all that steep, making it to the cabins would require even more effort on their part. If they did reach the cabins, it wasn't likely any phones would extend the reach of the lodge. Will suspected the Hunter would have taken care of that already. Once there, there would be nowhere to go but down.

"Over there," Cole said. He pointed toward the river behind Will. Will turned around and followed his friend.

There was a tent leaning against the brush in close proximity to the river. The exposed earth surrounding the tent was covered in muddy tracks.

"Someone was here recently," Will whispered. The three campers crept into the moonlight, drawing nearer to the tent.

It was then they spotted the man standing on the banks of the river. His back was turned to them. Dave's foot snapped a twig, and the man spun around. He was wearing a brown shirt, dark pants, and boots. Dave looked ready to bolt, but Will gestured for him to remain in place. The man didn't appear to be armed. Neither was he wearing the jacket or bandana the Hunter concealed himself with.

The man faced them for a moment, watching the three campers with a cautious gaze. Will stepped forward, and the other two followed uneasily. The stranger was standing against the bank, cut off from the tent by the campers. From the look of things, he'd been washing his hands in the river when they stumbled across him.

"Who are you?" Will asked. He looked around to make sure they were alone.

"My name is Bart," the man answered uneasily. He walked up the bank toward them. There was a gleam in his eye Will didn't like. "I'm out here camping, the same as you."

"Pardon me if I don't trust you," Will replied. "One of our friends was just shot to death on Whispering Reach."

Although the stranger wasn't wearing the same clothes as the killer, the Hunter could have changed his attire at any time. Will knew he was being paranoid, but something about Bart's demeanor troubled him.

"Why would anyone do something like that?" Bart asked flatly, holding up his hands in protest. He watched the others with interest.

"We're in danger," Cole interrupted. "All of us. We need to find shelter."

Will glanced at the flimsy tent. Bart was a sitting duck.

The stranger looked at them a while before nodding in agreement.

"Just let me get my things," he said, heading toward the tent. Will happened to glance back in the tent's direction just before Bart walked past them.

"Stop!" he shouted. He placed himself in Bart's way. Cole glanced up, alarmed. "Look," Will said.

Leaning against the tent was a shotgun. Bart gritted his teeth and gazed at the three men.

Will stared him down angrily. "Thought you'd pull a fast one on us?" Bart made no move to go for the weapon. "Dave, grab the gun." The heavy man snatched up the weapon and trained it on the stranger.

"Let's not be hasty," Bart said.

"Why do you have a gun?" Cole demanded. "What were you planning to do with it?"

Bart shook his head violently. "You've got the wrong idea. I didn't kill your friend."

"Then why the shotgun?" Will repeated. "Cole, search his tent. See what else he's hiding in there." There was silence as the law student pulled down the zipper and stepped inside Bart's tent. He emerged a few seconds later, holding another two-way radio and a handful of bullets.

"I found these inside the tent," he said, handing Will the shells. "There was also a written message from Ranger Fields along with the radio."

Will slid the shells into his pocket and took the shotgun from Dave. "You'd better start giving us some answers."

"It's not me, I swear," the man said. "I heard gunshots and went out to investigate. I've been here for a few days already."

"That's not good enough," Will said.

"I made it as far as the museum. There was a man inside the shed."

"Museum?" Cole asked.

"There's an old cemetery on the property," Will answered. "I learned about it when I started looking into the park." He turned his gaze back to Bart. "The man you saw. What did he look like?"

"He was about your height," the stranger answered. "He looked a little like you. He had black hair."

"Zack?" Cole asked, concern in his voice.

Will paused. If Zack was wandering around the cemetery, that meant he was still alive. The graveyard wasn't far from the recreation area, where they'd been when the Hunter attacked. Unless Bart could be in two places at once, it was unlikely he was the killer.

"Did he have a weapon?"

"Not that I could see. I tried to talk to him, but he ran the other way. Then I came back to the tent."

Will's eyes narrowed. "There's something you're not telling us."

Bart sighed. Will could tell the stranger was contemplating sharing delicate information. When he spoke again, it was with obvious reluctance.

"I was away from my tent most of the day. I've been hunting," he admitted. "That's why I had the gun."

"What do you mean?" Dave asked, not understanding.

"I was poaching," Bart clarified.

Now it all fit. Bart was the one who was shooting earlier in the day, the one Ron and Beth heard. When Zack saw Bart, he saw the gun and probably assumed the worst. Will eased up on the trigger.

"Can you take us to the museum?" Cole asked.

Will looked at his friend with shock. "Why would we want to go there?"

"We have to find Zack."

Will scowled. "Zack knows how to handle himself in the forest. We need to find shelter first." He looked Bart up and down. He didn't know the poacher and didn't trust him. "You're welcome to join us," he said, "but I'll be keeping an eye on you. I'll also hold onto this," he added, looking at the gun. Although he wasn't certain, it looked like Bart smiled at the words.

"The man who killed your friends," Bart said. "Was he wearing a necklace by any chance?"

"I'm not sure," Cole said. He looked at Bart curiously. "Why do you ask?"

"No reason," Bart replied. "When I arrived here, there was a man leaving the lodge wearing a necklace. Something about him didn't sit well with me."

***

The men's voices carried past the trees. Rodney Crowe stood just beyond the dirt trail overlooking the valley. They were close. He checked his device one more time. There were two hits coming from the valley. When he stalked them outside the recreation area, there was only one hit. There were more of them now.

Crowe smiled. Fractured as they were, the campers thought by grouping together, they could survive. They couldn't be more wrong. In the wilderness, it was every man for himself. Banding together only meant combining weaknesses, and they were plenty weak enough already. Crowe didn't even need the device to pursue the three campers. Their trail was all too easy to follow. He'd barely missed before with the arrows. He wouldn't miss again. Some of them would no doubt try to hide, which was why the tracking device was necessary. The killer was a man of his word. If they could last the night, he would let them go. They didn't know he could always find them.

The campers could try to escape. They might even get far. That rule was also a ruse. There was no escape from the park. The edge of Drifter's Folly was lined with traps and hidden dangers. If they took Beggar's Road or tried to return to the lodge, they would find another surprise waiting for them.

There was no way out.

CHAPTER NINE

ZACK STARED AT THE KNIFE. He moved slowly, careful not to upset the man holding it.

"Your friend mentioned there were two more of you," Ron said. "He never told us your names."

Beth remained silent. The worry on her face was palpable. Zack knew the situation looked bad. He was covered in Steve's blood, and there was no way to prove he was *not* the killer.

"Don't do anything you'll regret," Zack said. He backed away slowly, and a twig snapped under his weight. The hair on the back of his neck stood on end. Somewhere out there was the real killer.

"That blood on your shirt didn't come from you," Ron said.

"I was standing next to my friend when he was shot," Zack protested.

Ron's expression didn't change. It was clear that his nerves were getting the best of him, causing him to throw logic out the window.

"Maybe he's telling the truth," Beth said. The two men looked at her. "He was caught in the trap."

Zack nodded and seized on the point. "That's right. Why would I tie myself up?"

That gave Ron pause. He turned to Beth. "Maybe he was trying to trick us into letting our guard down. Or maybe he forgot where he put the trap. It's dark enough." There was doubt in Beth's eyes. "I won't let anyone hurt you," he finished.

"Then just let me go," Zack said. He held up his arms. "I'll disappear into the forest and you'll never see me again." He didn't want to be in the woods on his own, but it was better than the alternative.

"I'm not letting you out of my sight. If you are the killer, you've probably got some weapons stored nearby."

His logic didn't make sense. Even if that were true, there was no way anyone could get to the weapons in the first place with Ron standing guard over them.

The three people stood in silence, each looking anxiously at the other. Before anyone voiced another opinion, the two-way radio at Ron's belt roared to life.

"Hello?" a voice crackled through the static. The voice echoed again, saying something unintelligible.

"Honey, take it," Ron said, never taking his eyes off Zack. Zack admired the man's devotion to his girlfriend, but he needed a way out of this situation. "Switch channels," Ron added.

"Is someone there?" Beth asked. "Ranger Fields, is that you?"

For a moment, there was no response, and Zack feared the connection was severed, until the radio crackled again.

"This is Will Bradley. I'm with two of my friends and another camper. We're trying to raise Fields."

"Will?" Zack exclaimed. Ron raised his knife, but Zack ignored him. "Press the call button again," he said to Beth. She did as he asked. "Will, it's me. Tell them you know my voice."

"Thank God." Will sounded relieved. "We thought you were dead. The other guy who's with us said he saw you by the museum. We weren't sure he was telling the truth."

So that was the man with the shotgun, Zack thought. The killer wasn't the person who pursued him after all. So where was the murderer hiding?

"Are you all okay?"

"Yes," Will replied. "We were attacked near the recreation area and Dave was shot with an arrow. He's holding up well for the time being, all things considered. Don't go near that place. The payphone doesn't even work."

"So much for finding a phone," Ron muttered. He put his knife away again.

"Where are you?" Zack asked.

"In a valley near the river. What about you?"

Zack wasn't sure.

"We're on the Cemetery March Trail," Ron said. "At least we were when we ran into you."

"I think we're close to you," Will replied.

"If we head in the direction of Whispering Reach, we might find each other."

"What's your plan?" Will asked.

Zack considered their options. "The forest is rigged with traps. We need to get out of here. If we double back to the cliff, we can grab our keys and make for the lodge."

Will didn't answer for a moment. "That's an awfully large gamble to take," he finally said. "I think—"

Something cut him off.

"Will?" Zack asked, taking the radio from Beth. "Will?" he repeated.

"Hang on," Will said. "I thought I heard something."

The radio went silent. Zack looked at the others. A few seconds later, gunshots echoed through the night. Zack's face was etched in worry. He'd already lost so much. He couldn't lose his friends too. For the first time that evening, he felt a pang of despair. It was like a cloud had descended upon him. Something about the feeling was wrong, like a foreign consciousness stirring in his mind.

At that moment, Zack spotted a figure over Ron's shoulder. Ron followed his gaze and turned around, just as a man with a gun stepped into the moonlight. He was wearing a black bandana around his face and a dark jacket. It was the Hunter. In his hands was a rifle.

"Run!" Zack shouted.

A bullet exploded into the tree near his right shoulder. The three campers scurried into the brush, running away from the trail. It occurred to Zack the killer was herding them, pushing them in the direction he wanted them to go, but there was nothing to be done about it.

"Don't stop!" Ron shouted as he took Beth by the hand. Zack ran side-by-side with the couple across a level field. The tall trees were sparse, and the dry ground was flat. Suddenly, Ron fell to the ground. Zack turned his head. The bulky man had tripped over a wire.

"It's a trap!" Zack screamed. He grabbed Beth and pulled her out of the way. Ron scrambled to his feet as a large pile of lumber tumbled downhill their way. Another shot echoed through the night behind them. The killer was following closely. Zack could see his silhouette in the darkness. They were in a relatively open environment, and there were few places to hide.

He led Beth behind a tree. She almost cried out to Ron, but Zack clamped a hand against her mouth.

"Quiet," he said. Zack peered around the side of the tree. The noise created by the rolling lumber masked their location.

"Where's Ron?" she whispered urgently.

One of the enormous logs smashed into an old tree, causing it to snap in half. The collision was deafening. Zack spotted Ron on the ground, having barely missed being hit by the logs. After catching Ron's eye, Zack tried to signal to him to hide. Ron managed to take the hint, and crawled into the bushes nearby.

How did he find us? Zack thought.

He remembered the gunshots that rang out before he first saw the Hunter. Someone on Will's end of things had fired a weapon.

Zack was sure that it couldn't have been the killer. After all, they were the ones currently being pursued. So who had fired the gun?

He didn't have time to dwell on the thought. The killer walked through the forest, his gun held high as he searched for them. Beth almost screamed when the man walked past the bushes where Ron was hiding. Suddenly, the killer stopped. He turned, as if he could sense Ron, and swung his gun in Ron's direction.

"Ron!" Beth exclaimed.

The killer whirled around and fired. Zack pulled Beth back behind the tree.

Now we have to make a run for it.

"We have to go now," he whispered.

"I can't leave Ron," she protested.

"The killer is on his way here. We'll lead him away from Ron."

Beth rose to her feet reluctantly. Zack silently counted to three with his fingers, and the two rushed farther into the forest. Rather than remain hiding as the killer searched for them, Ron pushed himself up and raced in the same direction.

"This way," Zack whispered. He led Beth into the brush. Thorns and vines cut his skin, but they kept moving. The pair spilled out into another clearing. Beth was now outpacing him. Zack looked over his shoulder. The killer was nowhere in sight.

When Zack turned his gaze back to Beth, he stopped cold. Running blind, she didn't see the danger in front of her.

"Beth!" he shouted in a desperate attempt to get her attention.

It was too late. The ground opened up underneath her feet, and she started to fall into a pit. Zack dove to the ground and slid in her direction. He managed to catch her arm at the last moment. Her body collided with the soil wall. Zack felt an enormous strain on his left arm. He stared down at Beth. Her wide eyes were visible in the moonlight.

The killer had dug an enormous hole and covered it with leaves. Wooden spikes adorned the bottom of the hole. If the fall didn't kill her, the spears probably would have. When Zack tried to pull Beth up, his strength fled from him. He faltered, and she screamed.

"Beth!" he heard Ron shout.

A gunshot echoed over Ron's shoulder. The stocky man stumbled, and his foot tripped over another wire. Before Ron could move, a sharpened log swung down from a tree and impaled him. He was knocked into the air, and landed hard against a wide log.

Roaring from the pain of having to support Beth's weight, Zack slowly pulled her the surface.

"Don't look," Zack said. "Stay here." He crawled over to Ron. The man was breathing shallowly. Blood was already pouring from his wounds.

"Come on," Zack said. He tried to lift him, but Ron wouldn't budge. "We've got to get you somewhere safe."

As the words left his mouth, he knew they were impossible. Even if Ron's injuries weren't life threatening, moving him was unthinkable. Besides, the killer was still nearby.

Ron looked at Zack for a moment before his gaze settled on Beth.

"Get her out of here," he said weakly. He seized Zack's hand with surprising strength. "Keep her safe. Promise me."

The response was mechanic.

"I will."

"Go!"

Zack scrambled back and climbed to his feet. Beth was staring at Ron, sheer terror in her eyes. Her companion looked back at her with a pained expression.

Zack grabbed her gently by the shoulder. "We have to go."

"I'm not leaving Ron," she managed to mutter.

Zack pulled Beth to her feet over her protests. She cast one look back at Ron and followed him into the night.

***

As Ron sat against the log, he tried his best to ignore the pain. If there was time to get him to a hospital, he might have survived. Considering his current location, the prospect of that happening was remote. He sat there in silence for several minutes, fighting to stay conscious.

The brush rustled behind him, and the sound of footsteps echoed softly nearby. Peeking over the log, Ron caught a glimpse of the Hunter scanning the area for him. With a trembling hand, he reached down for the hunting knife at his belt.

The Hunter approached the log and lowered his gun. Gathering his courage, Ron jumped over the log and attacked with the knife. The killer kicked the wounded man in the side. Ron cried out in pain, and the Hunter grabbed Ron's wrist with his free hand and twisted it back. Ron screamed and dropped the knife. The killer's necklace spilled outside his jacket, revealing a deformed skull. Ron heard voices in his head just before the Hunter clubbed him with the rifle, and Ron fell to the ground.

***

The Hunter watched the twitching man for several moments before picking up the blade. As he finished his work, he listened for sounds of the man's companions.

Although the Hunter heard echoes, none came from any human source. He touched the thing around his neck with a gloved hand. Even in the darkness, it was a beautiful thing to behold. He called it a necklace, for that was the best word he had to describe it. The term didn't truly do the item justice.

Larger than his palm, the object was shaped in a circle. There was a layer of dark metal surrounded by a rocky exterior. Several grooves were carved into the rock, as if they were slots of some kind. In the heart of the circle was a monstrous skull. The Hunter kept the object tied around his neck at all times.

Sometimes, he thought others could sense the necklace's power, though never explicitly. The Hunter saw the necklace for what it really was: a window to a realm he couldn't fully comprehend. There were voices on the other side that spoke to him. They told him what to do and filled his head with hidden knowledge. Some of the voices were more powerful than others. There was a presence on the other side that never spoke to the Hunter. He could always feel the entity there, listening. The Hunter called the presence inside the necklace the Destroyer, for he had no other name for it.

Some people would consider him crazy. Maybe he was. The Hunter considered the possibility that there were no voices. Perhaps the necklace was just an ordinary piece of metal. He wondered if everything was coming from his own mind. He tried not to dwell on the subject. In the end, it didn't matter if the whispers came from some other realm or if they were his own. He couldn't ignore the dark impulses. He didn't want to. He was so much more than what he was when he found the necklace. With each life he took, his ability to understand the voices grew.

The Hunter didn't need to check the device in his jacket to know that the man's companions remained nearby. He stared down at the dead man lying at his feet. He was just getting started.

CHAPTER TEN

"IF WE DOUBLE BACK TO the cliff, we can grab our keys and make for the lodge."

Cole could tell from the looks on the others' faces that they were unsure how to respond to Zack's suggestion. He turned his eyes to Bart. The stranger stood between Dave and Will, the latter of whom continued to hold onto the gun. Cole still didn't trust the poacher, even if the man wasn't the one hunting them. There was something disconcerting about the man's movements, something shifty about him. From Will's expression, his friend shared the feeling.

Cole waited while Will pondered Zack's words. He wasn't sure why he looked to Will for leadership. Maybe it was that he was holding the gun, or maybe it was because Will was far more experienced than either of them. Whatever the case, Will had assumed control over the small group in their time of crisis. At the moment, Cole wasn't sure how he felt about that. He studied Will's eyes in the moonlight. There was a gleam there he'd never noticed before that was unsettling.

Even though they both shared many of the same classes in college, Cole was far closer to Zack than Will. It had always been that way, as far back as he could remember. Cole was studious and reserved, and Will was the polar opposite of that. They were able to bond over their shared course-load and some common interests, but there was no real depth to their relationship. Most of the time this superficial friendship worked fine. Zack bridged the personality difference between the two.

There were a few occasions when their friendship had been put to the test. They'd almost come to blows once over a girl Cole felt Will was trying to take advantage of. In the end Will had grinned that half-smile of his and said something to the effect that there would be other girls before walking away. Cole tried not to begrudge Will's success with women, but he did resent the way he treated them. There was a selfishness to Will most people couldn't see because of his outgoing nature. It was the same willingness to put himself first that Will displayed when he shouted to leave Dave behind. For now, Cole decided to keep his reservations to himself. He knew better than to judge someone going through a traumatic experience.

As he turned his attention back to the two-way radio, Cole thought of Zack, lost somewhere in the forest. Hearing his friend's voice again was surreal. Only moments ago he was convinced Zack was dead.

The wind shifted in the opposite direction, and Cole thought he heard footsteps in the distance. He looked up at the trees along the river. Cole stopped dead in his tracks. A shadow moved along the trees, watching them.

As soon as it had appeared, the shape was gone.

"That's an awfully large gamble to take," Will finally said. A rustling sound echoed in the dark. "I think—"

Will stopped. Cole knew he heard it too.

"Will?" Zack asked over the two-way radio. He said his friend's name again.

"Hang on," Will said. "I thought I heard something." He released the call button and motioned to the others to follow him. "Come on," he whispered. "It's not safe here."

Cole heard a clicking noise, and Bart stopped behind them. The poacher looked down. He was standing on a metal object buried in the ground. A flickering red light flashed.

"Don't move," Will said.

Cole pointed the light from his cell phone at the man's foot. "What's that?" Dave asked.

"It looks like some kind of mine," Cole said.

That was when the chaos broke out. An arrow sailed from above, hitting Bart in the back. When he fell forward, the ground exploded below him. Soil flew into the air, and smoke filled the night sky.

***

Closest to the blast, Dave was knocked against the forest floor, covered by leaves and dirt. As his vision blurred, he saw Cole struggling to rise from the ground next to Will, who appeared to be unconscious.

There was a large crater in the ground where Bart was standing only a few seconds ago. A scream rang out, and Dave spotted the poacher not far away. Because of the delay in the explosion, Bart had managed to avoid being blown to bits, but only just. He was crawling along the ground, futilely grabbing at the arrow embedded in his back.

Dave's ears were ringing.

"I can't find my glasses," he thought he heard Cole shout. Dave saw him feeling along the earth for the pair of lenses, which had been lost amidst the chaos unleashed by the landmine.

Dave pushed himself up and stumbled forward. His legs felt like jelly. The others were shouting something, only he couldn't hear them. Blood was dripping from his ears. Out of the corner of his eye, he saw Will begin to wake up.

Dave was already running when the arrow nailed him in the shoulder. He slid in the mud and landed on his knees just shy of the brush. His scream joined in the chorus of wails and moans coming from the others. Dave regained his footing and slipped into the forest. He would go to the cabins, like he wanted from the beginning. Maybe if he were on his own, the killer would have a harder time finding him.

***

Will blinked and saw a dark figure partially concealed by the trees standing on the hill above them. He wasn't sure, but he thought he could see a bow in the man's hands.

From his vantage point on the hill, the killer raised his bow.

Will crawled toward the shotgun on the ground. He reached for the weapon and missed, his hand falling short. Snarling, he reached out a second time. He was rewarded by the sensation of cold metal under his fingers. Will aimed the gun blindly in the direction of the trees and fired. The gun echoed loudly across the park.

The bullet missed the killer by a wide margin. Will saw him slide a hand into his jacket pocket and remove something that looked like a detonator.

That can't be good, he thought.

He saw Cole crawling along blindly in the valley. Without his glasses, he was legally blind. Will grabbed Cole and helped him to his feet.

"What's happening?" Cole asked. "Where's Dave?"

"He's gone," Will said. "We need to get out of here now."

Dave had vanished into the other side of the forest. From the look of things, he was headed toward the mountains.

Will didn't even want to think about how the killer found them again. They needed to get away.

"What about Bart?" Cole asked.

The wounded man was still crawling slowly away from the crater, moaning softly. Evidently Cole's ears continued to ring from the explosions, because he couldn't hear the poacher.

"He's dead," Will lied. If Cole thought there was a chance they could save Bart, he wouldn't leave without the poacher.

At that moment, dozens of red lights lit up the valley like Christmas. Will's mouth dropped open in horror. "Run!" he shouted, clutching the shotgun.

An explosion rocked the landscape, quickly followed by another. The two men scrambled through the forest, rocked by rattling blasts. Ripped from their roots, trees tumbled down and smashed against the earth. Debris rained down on them, and Will had difficulty remaining upright. He could only imagine how difficult things were for Cole.

He knew that somewhere out there, Zack was waiting for them. Will wished their roles were reversed, and Zack was the one under attack. Will had too much to live for. There were so many things he hadn't done yet.

"Come on!" he shouted to Cole, who lagged behind. "Just a little farther!"

They sped up and their trail led uphill in the direction of the river. The explosions ceased by the time they cleared the hill. Will cast a glance over his shoulder. The valley lay in ruins. Smoke covered the air.

He was glad he still held the shotgun. It made him feel safer. He was in control. As the pair slowed down, he led Cole away from the sound of the water. Unlike the sparsely populated trees of the valley, this portion of the forest was thick and musty. Cole stumbled in the darkness and hit the ground.

"What is it?" Will asked, keeping his eyes on alert.

"I can barely see," Cole said before sucking in a lungful of air. "I lost my glasses back there."

"We're not going back for them," Will said aggressively.

Cole looked at him like he hadn't intended to suggest such a thing. "What are we going to do now?"

"Survive," Will replied.

They were safe, for the moment. The killer's trap likely caused too much chaos for the man to follow them. Nevertheless, Will remained uneasy. That was twice the killer found them after they left Whispering Reach. Even if the man were an expert hunter, he tracked them down in only a few hours. Surely that should have been impossible. Something was wrong, only Will couldn't figure out what.

"We should try contacting Zack again," Cole said. "We need to band together. On our own, we're weak."

Why didn't I think of that? Will wondered angrily. He looked back at Cole. The law student probably couldn't even see him clearly. Will hoped his friend's blindness wasn't going to cause him problems.

He tried the radio. "Zack? Can you hear me?" There was no response.

"What about Dave? Didn't he have the walkie-talkie we took from Bart's tent?"

"It doesn't matter. There's no answer from anyone." Will tried Zack again. "Why isn't he answering? We're the ones who almost got killed back there."

***

"I'm sure Zack would answer if he could," Cole said defensively.

At least Zack was alive. It was one small comfort at the moment. Cole wondered how his friend was managing the stress. He remembered walking into the lodge earlier with Zack and felt a pang of pity for him. When he tried talking to Zack in the cave, he briefly thought his friend was going to open up. The moment quickly faded, just like all the times before.

Had he failed Zack as a friend? Cole tried his best to help Zack recover from the pain of Lily's death. Anger festered inside his friend until it now threatened to explode. Nothing seemed able to help suppress that rage. Cole understood Zack couldn't find peace on his own.

"I said we need to get a move on it," Will said. Cole looked up at him, unable to discern his facial features. "I can't afford to have you lose focus."

"Sorry," Cole replied. "I was thinking of Zack."

"We need to think about ourselves for now."

Will was right. Cole reproached himself for thinking ill of Will before. His friend had probably saved his life in the valley. It wasn't Will's fault the others were dead—it was the killer's. They needed to work together.

"Zack was right about one thing," Cole said as the two made their way through the forest. The lack of vision was a problem, but in the dark he couldn't see very well anyway. "We need a plan."

"We're not about to try getting back to the tent on our own." The forest lay still around them, in contrast to the deafening destruction they had fled from.

"I agree. If we can't find Zack, it's too risky." After a slight pause, he continued. "There might be another way."

Will stopped. "What way?"

Cole carefully removed his cell phone from his pocket. Its light illuminated the darkness for small interval until it faded after a period of disuse.

"We don't have to escape. We just need to get close enough to get service."

Will considered the idea for a moment. "That could work."

They could feasibly reach the lodge, perhaps by force if necessary. After all, Will was carrying the shotgun. A well-placed phone call would have the park swarming with police before the Hunter had a chance to finish his work.

"Since the killer was near the river, we know he's not blocking the path to the lodge," Will added.

"Exactly. And if Zack and the others meet us on the way, we can still try to get the keys."

Will seemed about to reply when an unmistakable sound echoed through the quiet forest. It was an engine. Could it be?

They had heard the same noise earlier in the day, long before the madness began. It was the sound of an ATV.

"Fields," Cole whispered. As the noise of the engine grew louder, the wind picked up again. The sound of the engine started to vanish.

"No!" Will roared. "Come on!" he shouted to Cole.

The two men took off in the direction the sound came from. They raced down a leafy hill, running as fast as they could. Even if the radio wasn't working, maybe Fields heard the shots and came after all. If so, there was a chance the ranger could drive them to safety.

To Cole's horror, the sound continued to drift away.

"Fields!" Will shouted, abandoning any effort to remain silent.

Cole lumbered down the hill above him, slowed by his lack of vision. The sound was now almost out of earshot. As a last-ditch effort, Will stopped and discharged the shotgun into the air. It might bring the killer in their direction, but surely Fields would have to hear it. Cole caught up with him, and the two men continued running, hoping for a rescuer to materialize in the woods.

The sound of the engine finally died away. Cole kept racing blindly, unable to see anything other than his friend's image.

Without his glasses, he never saw the shimmering metal buried in the leaves.

Metal snapped up, and what felt like knives ripped into his leg just above the foot. Cole's scream echoed across the night sky.

Will turned around in time to see his friend go down. Cole whimpered on the ground, his face marked by an expression of agony. He had stepped on a bear trap.

***

The lonely cabin was cast in shadow by the mountain peak above. There were other cabins strewn across the mountains, but each was located almost a mile away from the next. Each cabin sat in solitude, waiting for a new visitor to set foot inside. The cabin closest to the injured man was fairly large, an impressive wooden structure resting under the pale light of the moon. Built over fifty years ago, the cabins had languished in disuse for a long while. Despite the lack of customers, they remained looked after in case someone came looking to rent.

The front door was locked. A trembling hand gripped the doorknob and slipped off, leaving a bloodstain in its place. Dave was covered in blood. Most of it was from his wounds, although he was certain some of Bart's blood was mingled with his own. Dave slammed his body against the doorframe. It buckled under his weight. Moonlight spilled into the musty interior, and Dave stumbled inside the cabin. Exasperated, he fought the urge to sink to his knees.

He retained the presence of mind to check to see if the cabin was unoccupied. There were no signs to the contrary. In fact, the entire building was practically bare. There was no phone inside, not that he expected to find one. Dave glanced out one of the dark windows, searching for the man who was after his friends. From what he could see, he was alone.

I made it, he thought. The others were out there scurrying in the dark. They were wrong to try to escape. He warned them. Dave took two steps and had to press his hand against the wall not to fall. He was dizzy from the loss of blood. It didn't matter. Here he could be safe. The cabin was located in the mountains, which lined the boundaries of the park. While the killer was hunting the others in the forest, Dave could wait for morning or rescue, whichever came first. After all, the Hunter had promised them he would spare anyone who lasted until morning.

Dave searched for a place to hide. He passed through the empty hall and walked slowly up the steps. No one would look for him here. He found a closet in one of the rooms on the upper floor. Dave crawled inside the closet, closed the door behind him, and peered out the blinds. The room was empty. He no longer had anything to fear. He fumbled in his pocket for the two-way radio. Dave turned it off so it wouldn't make a sound that might alert anyone nearby to his presence. If he needed it, he would have it just in case. He briefly considered attempting to contact the others, but decided it was too risky.

His shoulder throbbed with pain. He had broken the arrow shaft, but the tip remained buried in his flesh. It was a stinging, constant pain.

Dave could feel himself losing consciousness. He decided not to fight it. He was alone, and he was so tired. Why not give in? He was safe now. Dave closed his eyes. A few seconds later, he was asleep.

CHAPTER ELEVEN

SHE WAS SO FULL OF life. The more Zack grew to know Lily, the more he realized his life before her was merely scraping by. With Lily, he enjoyed almost every second. There was always a new experience to be had, a new adventure to set out on. Almost four months into their relationship, she once spontaneously dragged him along on a ten-hour drive all the way to the coast. It wasn't until later that he saw another side to her. There was brightness in her eyes that he remembered even in her worst bouts with depression. Now that light had been put out, and the world was darker for it.

Zack felt dirty. His clothes were stained with blood, mud, and sweat. He was no longer aware of the time. It felt like an eternity had passed since he first saw the killer moving outside their tent. He wished he'd done something when he had the chance. Instead, Steve was dead and they were scattered at the mercy of the Hunter's deadly game.

"I don't know where we are," he said finally.

Zack glanced at Beth, who gave no response. He repeated himself in case she hadn't heard him, but didn't make a difference. Sighing, he trekked across the leaves and joined her on the ground. They were surrounded by mounds of gravel in front of a tunnel of some kind. Two rusted bulldozers rested nearby, both far from operational. The area was somewhat walled off by a broken mesh fence. Dozens of tree stumps covered the area. It looked like a mining or logging operation of some kind, though he wasn't sure. The site wasn't on any of the maps he'd seen.

He almost put a hand on Beth's shoulder, but drew it back.

"I know what it's like to lose someone," he said. The words felt hollow. Not long ago, Cole said them to him. Zack knew firsthand they were of little comfort.

Whatever effect the words had on her, his voice stirred Beth from her trance.

"We should go back," she said. "Ron needs our help."

There were tears in her eyes, and Zack was struck with the overwhelming need to wipe them away. Instead, he rose and started pacing. The anger at the unfairness of it all welled under the surface.

When he looked at her again, he saw the realization in her eyes. Ron wasn't coming back. Even if the Hunter hadn't caught up to him, the trap had done its work too well.

"Ron wanted you to focus on staying alive," Zack said. "That's what we're going to do."

Beth nodded and stopped sniffling. Maybe she was stronger than she looked. Under the open light of the moon, she no longer looked anything like Lily. Zack wasn't sure how he made the mistake before.

His promise to Ron hung in the air like an unfinished sentence. Zack didn't know how, but he would keep his word.

I won't fail her, he thought. *Not like I failed Lily.*

Beth looked around, as if only now aware of their surroundings. "Where are we?"

"I'm not sure." Zack stared at the black hole dug into the mountain. "There are a couple of caves across Drifter's Folly. This could be one of them, or some kind of mining operation." The truth was, he didn't care. They were still trapped inside the confines of the park. That was all he needed to know.

She pointed at the bulldozers. "Do those work?"

Zack shook his head. "I already checked." He leaned against a pile of lumber and tried radioing his friends. Once more the radio had fallen silent.

"What's wrong?" Beth asked. Even in the darkness, she was perceptive.

"Nothing," Zack started. "I heard shots before we were attacked, coming from the place where my friends were calling. I'm not sure, but while we were running I thought there were explosions in the distance."

Beth looked confused. "I don't understand."

"If the Hunter was chasing us, why was there any shooting going on at all on my friends' end? The man can't be in two places at once."

"It doesn't matter," Beth said. "We have to get out of here either way." There was a lull in the conversation.

They were both thinking the same thing. *How?*

"What about the lake?" she asked suddenly. "It flows into rivers and creeks. If we could find a boat, we could take it back to the park entrance."

"We'd be sitting ducks in a canoe, even if we could find one."

Beth shook her head emphatically. "Not a canoe. There are motorboats here somewhere. Ron and I saw the dock on the drive to Drifter's Folly."

For a moment Zack started to hope. He remembered seeing a sign for a boating rental area earlier.

"I think I know what you're talking about it, but I don't remember where it was."

"The dock was only a few miles south of the lodge." Beth's expression quickly darkened. "I think all the boats were covered. I doubt they see much use this time of year."

Zack hadn't thought of that. There were so few campers in the park, there weren't likely to be any motorized boats just sitting nearby. The Hunter picked his time perfectly.

That doesn't mean the boats wouldn't be of use, he thought, *if we get that far.* At the moment, there were other matters to consider.

"Don't forget my friends," he added hastily. "We have to see if they're okay."

"What if we can't find them?"

Steve's face flashed before his eyes. Zack saw an image of Lily in the casket, her face locked in a lifeless expression so unlike her.

"Are you all right?" Beth looked concerned.

"I'll be fine," he said, a bit too forcefully.

Snap out of it, he ordered himself.

"We can start by finding one of the trails. We'll follow it back to Whispering Reach. If we can't find them over the radio, the others will know to meet us there."

"Why not stay here?" she asked. Beth looked up at the mountains towering over them. Zack spotted at least two cabins looming in the distance. "We can hide in the tunnel."

"A tunnel would be the worst place to hide," Zack said. "Once you go inside, you're cornered. There's no way out. I wouldn't go there unless there wasn't another choice."

Beth was quiet. "I don't want to go back there," she whispered, staring into the forest. "I'm afraid."

Zack didn't blame her. Normally innocuous, the trees had taken on a sinister appearance. The once-beautiful landscape was twisted into something far more horrifying. Going back into the forest would mean voluntarily returning to the trap-covered labyrinth of darkness constructed by the Hunter.

"So am I," Zack said, "but we don't have a choice."

Even so, he made no move to compel her to rise. He wouldn't force her to move. If Beth wanted to remain there, he would stay also. She was counting on him, and he suddenly found himself with a reason to stay alive.

"The person you lost," Beth said. "Who was it?"

The wind blew around him, and this time his voice was like a whisper.

"Someone I loved." He trailed off slowly. That was when he heard the engine. "Do you hear that?" he asked, alert.

"What?" Beth asked. She craned her head to one side as the noise grew louder.

"I think it's a motor," Zack said. Beth jumped to her feet. "It could be help."

"Or it could be the killer."

Zack frowned. "Stay close to me," he said softly. "Let's go."

Together they headed back into the dense forest, pursuing the sound of the engine.

"It's getting closer," Beth said when they passed a creek. Zack still didn't know where they were. If they could locate the source of the sound, maybe it wouldn't matter. He ran down a hill and almost slipped in the mud.

"Over here," Zack said.

A large form sprang into view as he stepped from behind a tree. When he approached, Zack could see the shape more clearly under the beam of his flashlight. He was almost certain it was Austin Fields' all-terrain vehicle. Although the motor was still running, the vehicle was flipped over on its side. There were skid marks on the ground where the tires had left a trail.

"What happened?" Beth asked. She knelt down and turned off the engine.

"This is the park ranger's vehicle," Zack whispered. He was crestfallen. They were on the verge of being rescued only a few seconds ago.

"How long do you think it's been here?" she asked.

"Not long, I'd guess. We probably just missed him."

"Two of the tires are flat," Beth said. Zack pointed his flashlight at the tires. There were two large tears in the rubber. "He must have hit something," she said.

Zack doubted the ranger's accident was coincidence. More likely it was by the killer's design. Now Fields was also drawn into the Hunter's game, if he even remained alive.

"What do you think happened to him?"

Beth didn't bother to reply.

Zack stared down at the wreckage. The ATV was of no use to them in its current condition. Having fled from the relative safety of the quarry, the two were lost again. Zack needed to find a trail quickly. Whispering Reach couldn't be too far way.

When he looked toward the creek, he froze. There were footprints in the mud leading away from the vehicle.

***

Cole Wallace's father was a hero. That's how he would always remember him. Brandon Wallace was everything his son wanted to be. A towering giant of a man, Brandon's long hours as a police officer never prevented him from tucking Cole into bed every night. When the shy, small boy found himself picked on by neighborhood kids, it was his father who put a stop to it. Moreover, everyone else respected Brandon too. A deacon in his church, Cole's father was always willing to lend a helping hand to someone in need.

Cole's fondest memories were of his father reading to him before bed. He especially loved the comics his father bought him. Cole's favorite was Daredevil, a hero who was also a blind lawyer by day. Since he was legally blind without his glasses, Cole identified with the costumed vigilante. He hoped that when he grew older, he could emulate his two heroes. When Brandon Wallace was diagnosed with pancreatic cancer Cole's sophomore year of high school, Cole's life came crashing down around him. He watched his physically powerful father slowly waste away before his eyes.

Through it all, Brandon Wallace never lost hope. Even when Cole or others were angry or fearful, Brandon never succumbed to despair. When his father finally passed away, Cole decided to pursue a career in law to honor his memory. Whenever things grew difficult, he always looked to his father's example.

As he lay prostrate in the darkness of the forest, Cole could no longer picture his father's image. All he could feel was pain. He tried to scream again, but no sound came out. His throat was raw, though that was the least of his problems. He couldn't bring himself to look at his leg.

***

Will didn't know what to do. Unless he could find a way to get Cole out of the trap, they were stuck, just like the killer no doubt intended when he planted the traps. He bent down on one knee and inspected the damage. Cole flinched away from his touch.

"Relax," he said soothingly. "I'm just looking. I'm not going to try anything yet."

There was a snap in the woods behind them. Will looked up quickly. Was it merely the sound of the forest, or something more insidious?

His nerves were on edge. He glanced back at the area above Cole's foot. The trap was designed for something far larger than a human, and it had done a lot of damage. The bone was probably broken. Will couldn't tell. The limb was definitely mangled. Unlike Dave's injury, this wound seemed far more serious. Even if he could free Cole, there was no guarantee they were going to make it far before the killer closed in on them.

"You're handling this pretty well," Will added, trying to keep his friend—and himself—calm. The statement also happened to be true. Cole was far calmer than seemed possible. Will couldn't imagine his reaction if their circumstances were reversed. Cole wasn't even wearing boots to begin with, which made matters even worse.

Maybe the injury isn't as bad as it looks, Will thought. It was certainly possible, given the darkness.

A twig snapped again. This time, Will started to panic.

"I've got to get you out of here," he said. Will gritted his teeth and tried prying the metal jaws apart. The trap didn't even budge. He tried a second time. Again, no success. Will gazed back at the woods, half expecting the killer to come tearing through the brush, gun in hand. He didn't know what to do. Will fidgeted around in his pocket and found the hunting knife he brought with him. He pulled it out, and the blade gleamed in the darkness.

Cole's eyes widened. "What's that for?" From the sound of his voice, he already knew the answer.

"I'm going to try to cut you out," Will said. His tone was casual, as if speaking of a subject as mundane as the weather.

"No," Cole said. He tried to move, but couldn't. "There has to be another way."

"There isn't," Will insisted. He was coming unglued from the stress. "Now hold still." He grabbed the bloody leg and held it in place against Cole's objections. Will steeled himself against the painful expression on his friend's face. He held the knife inches from Cole's leg. His hand was shaking badly. Will mustered his focus and slid the blade into flesh. Blood spurted everywhere, covering his clothes. Cole screamed louder than ever.

This isn't going to work, Will realized.

He cleaned the blade and returned it to his pocket. Rising from his crouched position, he took a few steps back and tried to assess the situation with a clear head. What could he do? This was nothing he ever trained for. The killer was out there somewhere, and every second Will tarried the man might be coming closer. Will took another step back. Cole probably couldn't even see him, considering his eyesight. His heart raced. If he couldn't free Cole, maybe he should try to find a place to hide. It wasn't right for both of them to die. If Cole lived, he would understand.

"Let's both try it together," Cole said. His voice sounded stronger than before, which was a good sign. "One more time."

"Okay," Will replied. "We'll do it at the same time. On the count of three."

He counted to three, and the two men pulled at the trap. To Will's surprise, the rusted metal began to move. Inch by inch, the teeth pulled back from Cole's skin. It was hard work, and Will almost lost his grip once or twice, but in the end Cole was able to slip his mangled leg out of the trap.

"Someone is looking out for you," Will said. It was a rare instance of good fortune on a luckless night. He helped Cole to the creek, where he washed the leg in the water. Will winced when he saw the injury under the moonlight. It looked even worse than he thought.

"Thank you," Cole said, clutching onto him with a tight grip.

"Don't mention it," Will said. He couldn't bring himself to look Cole in the eyes, not after he'd been willing to leave him. He felt a pang of guilt. "This isn't the trip I promised you guys."

"I think my leg will be okay," Cole said reassuringly. Will couldn't believe it. How could Cole be so calm when he was clearly suffering? "I'm just glad you didn't leave me."

"What do you mean?"

"With me stuck there, I thought you might get cold feet."

"The thought never crossed my mind," he lied. Will went to work trying to cover Cole's wound. After ripping his shirt, he made a makeshift bandage and wrapped it tightly against his friend's skin. Blood seeped through the cloth almost instantly, but it was the best he could do with what was available. Will studied his friend. Now that he had saved Cole, he hoped he wouldn't regret it. It was bad enough before when Cole was without his shoes or glasses. Now the man was not only blind, he was practically crippled.

They remained sitting at the edge of the creek for several minutes. Will was left unsure of the path forward. He'd staked his hopes on rescue.

"Where do you think the engine was coming from?" Cole asked. "Do you think it was really Fields?"

"If the police were coming, there would have been more of them." He looked away. "Why didn't he hear my shot?"

"Maybe he did hear it," Cole said. "Maybe he's out looking for us."

Always the optimist, Will thought. Even blind and injured, Cole still searched for the bright side of things. For some reason it angered Will. Sometimes things really were too bleak. Sometimes there was no light to be found. Only Cole hadn't seemed to get the message, even when reality went out of its way to deliver it.

"What about Zack?"

"He and the others are probably halfway to Whispering Reach by now. They'll have heard the explosions. If they hurry, they can get the keys and reach the lodge before the killer finds them."

Cole's voice was firm. "They wouldn't leave us."

Will stared at the water with a blank expression.

"Wouldn't they? We would, if we were in their position."

"No, we wouldn't."

Will didn't share Cole's optimistic outlook, but he was sure of one thing. He was going to find a way to survive—no matter what. Nothing and no one would stand in the way of that. He grabbed the gun and rose to his feet.

"Come on," he said, extending a hand. "We need to move along."

Although Cole grunted a little when he was on his feet again, he bore the pain of his injury well. He hobbled along, occasionally leaning on Will for support.

"What's that?" Cole asked. He gestured to an almost invisible path under the trees. Will's mouth fell open.

"The trail," he said, amazed his friend had spotted the path, considering his lack of vision. Will recognized their position instantly. It was Shatter Creek Trail. They were back where they started.

He ran ahead of his friend and peered through the trees. Whispering Reach loomed miles away, their tent hidden somewhere above.

CHAPTER TWELVE

1:42 AM

H E ARRIVED LATE, HALF-EXPECTING COLE to have vanished. Instead, his friend was waiting patiently at a table near the back of the restaurant. From the moment he looked Cole in the eye, Zack realized his friend knew it was only at the last second he decided to come at all. As always, Cole never brought it up.

"Hi," Zack said stiffly, acknowledging the formality of greeting. The mechanical gesture was all he had to give. He'd been sleepwalking through his life for so long he'd lost the willingness to observe most social niceties. Zack caught a glimpse of himself in a mirror on the wall. He looked rough.

"Right back at you," Cole said. "It's good to see you. I've been trying to get in touch for a while."

That was an understatement. Zack managed to avoid seeing his friends for weeks, but there were only so many times he could turn Cole down. Always persistent, Cole continued to make plans even after Zack missed each scheduled get together. Although Zack wished Cole would take the hint, a part of him admired his friend's determination.

"Sorry," he replied flatly. "I've been kind of busy."

Cole nodded and met his eyes with a knowing look, and then his friend broke into a smile.

"Well, I'm starving. How about something to eat?" He studied the menu. "What looks good?"

Zack looked it over briefly. In his current mood, nothing looked particularly appetizing. "I don't know."

Cole raised an eyebrow. "Zack Allen, world-class baker, unsure of what he wants to eat? This is a first."

Zack clenched his jaw. He felt his friend was judging him silently. That Cole of all people would do so only made him angrier.

"What do you want me to say?" he demanded, dropping the menu. Zack felt his fist clench. "I shouldn't have come." He started to rise, but found he couldn't walk out on his friend. Something made him stay.

"I'm so sorry," Cole said. His voice was genuine, moving even. Here he was trying to reach out, and Zack was slapping one of his only friends away. The right thing to do would have been to apologize. Instead, Zack grew angrier.

"Next you'll be telling me that it wasn't my fault," he snapped. The bitter words sounded foreign, like they were coming from somewhere else. "You'll say there was nothing I could do."

Cole shook his head. "That's not why I'm here."

Zack's voice broke. "Then why are you here?"

"What happened to Lily…nothing I can do can take that pain away. I'm always here if you want to talk about it, but that's up to you."

"Nothing *happened* to Lily. She killed herself."

And it's my fault, he thought silently.

At this, Cole was visibly shocked. "This isn't you, Zack. You've let your pain fill you with hate. If you don't find something else to fill that void, it'll take you to a place you don't want to be."

"How do you know?" Zack snapped.

"Because I know what it's like to lose someone."

Zack remembered hearing stories about Cole's father, the man who inspired him to become a lawyer. He hung his head and sat quietly.

"The pain is the only thing I have left of her." The admission was self-deflating.

"It doesn't have to be. Come with me to church on Sunday. Maybe you'll see for yourself."

Zack sighed. "Not this again."

"God still has a plan for you, Zack."

"You can't tell me Lily's death was part of a greater purpose."

Cole looked down at the table. "I don't claim to understand everything. There's good and evil in the world. Lily's death wasn't God's fault, the same way it wasn't your fault."

"Even if God was out there, why should I trust someone who stood by and let Lily die anyway?"

"Because He loved her enough to die for her, and you. God is the only thing big enough to fill the hole inside of you. Please, Zack. Come with me on Sunday."

There was silence at the table. "I can't," Zack finally said. "I just can't."

"Well, the offer is always on the table if you change your mind. Now what do you say we order something?"

Zack felt relieved that Cole didn't press the issue and had tactfully changed the subject. To his surprise, he actually enjoyed the meal. The two of them made small talk and discussed everyday events for almost an hour. Zack almost forgot about Lily during that time, though she never quite left his side. When the check came, he was suddenly aware of all the other people surrounding them. He felt cramped, smothered.

"Thanks for the invitation," he said. "I had a good time."

Cole's face grew instantly serious. "Let's do it again sometime."

"I'm not sure," Zack replied shakily.

"I'm not giving up on you. You've cut yourself off from the world, from your friends. There are people who care about you.

I've heard Will is even trying to organize a camping trip aimed at getting you back into the real world."

Zack perked up. "Really?" Although he felt reluctant to leave the comfortable safety of his routine, the possibility was intriguing. He left the restaurant with a lot to think about.

Beth touched his shoulder, and Zack felt himself pulled into the present.

"Those tracks are fresh."

Zack turned around. There was clear unease on Beth's face, and for good reason. There was no sign of Fields near the wrecked vehicle other than the footprints. Zack had no way of knowing if the footprints belonged to Fields or to the killer.

"They lead north," he said, scanning the moist earth with his flashlight.

Beth grabbed his arm. "Maybe we should follow them."

"What if we end up finding the wrong person at the other end of them?" he asked, tension in his voice. He switched the flashlight off.

"You heard the gunshots. Fields carries a gun. He could keep us safe."

You mean he could do a better job of keeping you safe, Zack thought. *Better than me.* He didn't blame her. She didn't know him at all, and Fields was a park ranger. Still, he promised Ron he would keep Beth safe, and Zack planned to do so.

"We could be headed into the belly of the beast. Even if these footprints belong to Fields, there's no way of telling if he's still alive."

"We can't just sit here and do nothing."

On that, he agreed with her. Zack slowly followed the footprints away from the water with Beth following close by. The tracks led away from a nearby trail.

"We're close to Whispering Reach," Zack whispered. The two peeked outside the forest through the brush. "About a half-mile,

I'd say. Following these footprints shouldn't lead us away from the trail. In case the others are coming, we should try and reach the cliff first."

Seeing that he'd conceded the argument, Beth let him lead the way farther into the woods. Following the footprints gave them something to do, along with a sense of purpose.

A low rumble sounded overhead. Unlike the gunfire they'd heard previously, this noise was from nature. They were moving north, and the light should have been growing stronger as the pair approached Whispering Reach. Instead, the forest continued to darken. Zack watched the sky. Clouds were beginning to spread, as if to shield the heavens from the horror unfolding below. When he and the others first made camp, the sky was clear. From the look of things, a storm was on the way.

We need to reach the cliff quickly, he thought. Deadman's Drop would be treacherous in the rain. He didn't know how long they had until the storm hit, but he didn't want to take any risks.

Beth outpaced him before coming to a sudden stop. She looked in both directions.

"Give me your flashlight," she said. Zack tossed the flashlight to her. The problem was obvious. The farther they moved from the damp ground near the creek, the drier the land became. The muddy tracks left by the person who crawled out of the wreckage were gone.

Beth switched on the flashlight and searched for anything that would indicate the traveler's path. There was nothing that might point out a direction they should go. Fields could have gone anywhere. Zack was about to suggest continuing toward the cliff when he heard a sound behind him. Something was moving in the woods not far from where they were.

"Turn off the flashlight," he said urgently.

The beam disappeared. He grabbed Beth's hand and led her in the darkness.

The sound was getting louder. Someone else was following the footprints. Zack pulled Beth off the path. He could feel her trembling.

"Quiet," he whispered. Zack wrapped an arm around her shoulder as they concealed themselves in the brush. "Stay calm." Her breathing was loud and quick.

Not long after, the pair heard footsteps nearby. Leaves rustled in the wind, and faint thunder rumbled again.

Maybe it's Fields, Zack thought. *Maybe he doubled back and heard us.* His gut told him otherwise. Dry grass crunched under a pair of black boots.

Slowly, the killer stepped into view. Zack saw Beth's eyes grow wide. He clamped a hand over her mouth, unable to tear his eyes away from the figure. The man's face remained masked by the bandana. There was a bow strapped to his back, though at the moment he wasn't holding any weapon in his hands. As Zack watched the figure advance, something didn't sit right with him. There was something different about the killer than when the man held a knife against his throat. Zack couldn't put his finger on the difference, but it was there all the same.

The Hunter was wearing goggles of some kind. Zack and Beth were hidden just out of sight, concealed by the bushes below, but they couldn't stay hidden forever. The murderer would find them if he searched long enough. Zack remembered the sour smell of the man's breath against his face. Beth was closing her eyes now, shaking more than ever. He held her even tighter. Why wasn't the killer moving on?

A few seconds later, the man removed his goggles. The murderer reached into his jacket, and Zack feared the worst. Rather than pull out a weapon, the man removed some kind of device. The figure switched the device on, and the glow of the screen illuminated the masked face. Zack craned his neck, trying to get a better look. What was the killer doing? The device was small, almost the size of a cell phone. Before Zack could learn anything further, the masked figure turned the device off and returned it to his jacket. When he pulled his hand free of his jacket again, it was clutching a pistol.

The figure lifted his head and inhaled, as if sniffing the air. He turned, directly facing the bushes where the pair was hiding. Zack couldn't tell in the growing darkness, but the killer appeared to be looking right at them. Zack's body screamed at him to run. It took all of his effort to remain still. The murderer took two steps forward. He was practically standing right on top of them. Zack froze. It was too late to move now. There was nowhere to go. His eyes moved down from the masked face to the gun, which hung loosely in the air.

Lily, he thought, bracing for the end. *I'm sorry.*

The thunder sounded again. The murderer looked at the sky and took a step back. His gaze moved to the ground, where he studied the last footprint for several minutes before marching east. He was headed toward Dire Lake. His footsteps eventually receded into the night.

Zack and Beth remained in place for what felt like hours until they were sure the killer wasn't coming back. Beth slumped forward and pressed her face against his shoulders. Zack didn't know how to react until she burst out crying. Tears poured down her face. He held her as she sobbed and made no move to get up.

"It's okay," he said softly, brushing her hair. "It's going to be okay, Lily." Either she didn't notice that he called her by the wrong name, or she chose to ignore it. They sat there like that for several minutes, surrounded by the sounds of the storm.

***

Rodney Crowe tried not to be impatient. It wasn't yet two in the morning. The night was still young. There was all the time in the world and plenty of potential victims scurrying about like rats. All the same, he was starting to feel uneasy. He had excelled in tracking his prey so far, but he couldn't escape the feeling he'd just let some slip through his fingers. The device was never wrong.

The clouds had appeared from nowhere, and he was unsure how rainfall would change the game. Crowe chided himself. There was no need for worry. Everything was going smoothly. The chaos inspired by his minefield in the valley was playing out nicely. The campers were divided, injured, or dead. Even so, there was much work left to do.

He stepped deftly over a pile of dry leaves and found himself looking at the lake. It continued sparkling in the faint moonlight, oblivious to the gathering clouds.

"You're exposed," a voice whispered behind him.

Crowe swore and turned around slowly. A handgun was pointing directly at his head.

"You should know better," the voice said.

As Crowe watched, the Hunter stepped into the light and lowered his weapon.

"I was wondering when I'd run into you," Crowe said. He searched the other man's black eyes for a hint of what was going on inside the man's mind. Like always, the eyes conveyed nothing. "I saw the ATV near the creek."

"Two of the campers were following the footprints, looking for Fields," the Hunter said. He touched the chain around his neck. Crowe had noted the Hunter's obsession with the necklace, though he chose not to mention it. "I've been tracking them." He held up a blade covered in blood. "After I took care of one of their friends."

"They'll be reunited with him soon enough."

Before Crowe could continue, the other man held up a hand to silence him. Both men were dressed identically.

"They're *mine*," the Hunter said, practically hissing. Crowe fell silent. "The man knows his way around the woods. He should prove interesting. Besides," he said with a sneer, "you already passed them by." The Hunter gestured to the goggles around his neck. "Have you forgotten how to use those?"

Crowe scowled. He knew he'd been close. He'd missed his chance. "There are plenty of them to go around. Let's not fight."

"No, that comes later."

For now, they would go their separate ways. They wouldn't pursue the same victims until later in the game. That was their custom. He held up two fingers.

"That makes two," he said. "Counting the man in the tent."

Crowe always felt the first kill shouldn't count, but that was the way the game was played. Underneath the bandana mask, he smiled.

"I blew one of them to pieces earlier," he said, "and shot another in the back. If he's still alive, I'll find him."

There was a flash of lightning over the lake, and thunder echoed overhead. When Crowe looked back at the forest, the Hunter had vanished. Crowe licked his lips and returned to the forest. There were no strict rules to the game, not for them anyway. They were the ones in control. Rules were for those who were hunted. Together, they would kill them all.

Crowe's hike turned upward. He had one little chore to complete before returning to Dire Lake. He knew what the campers were planning. They thought they could return to the lodge to their cars and escape. That would be the last mistake they would ever make.

CHAPTER THIRTEEN

2:13 AM

IT WAS GOING TO RAIN. Will felt it in his bones. It was only a matter of when. If they didn't reach the cliff before the storm hit, navigating through the forest would prove impossible. They would be exactly where the killer wanted them.

He turned to Cole. Though he put up a brave front, the wounded man was slowing down. "Are you all right?"

"I'll live." Cole winced as he mouthed the words.

Will shrugged. If Cole wasn't going to linger on his wounds, neither would he. Cole was keeping up with him for the moment, and that was enough. Will didn't want to think about what might happen if that changed. He didn't relish the idea of parting ways with his friend. It wasn't merely out of concern for Cole. Will didn't want to find himself alone in the forest.

The sky had grown even darker with the arrival of the storm front, if that was even possible. Will could barely see. "Check your cell phone again."

His friend squinted at the screen. "There's still no service." Cole returned the phone to his pocket.

Will sighed, frustrated. "Do you mind if I use it to shine some light down the trail?"

Cole shook his head. "I think we should try to conserve the battery."

That irritated Will. He'd gone out of his way to take care of Cole. The least his friend could do was let him use the phone for a little light. Each time Will thought his eyes had adjusted to the dark, the night seemed to swell with a new influx of blackness.

That was the main reason he was reluctant to leave Cole behind. Will didn't want to be on his own in the night. He clutched the shotgun tighter. The killer could be anywhere, hiding behind a tree or under the brush. The thought sent chills running down his spine.

When he was a young boy, Will was terrified by darkness. He slept with a nightlight until he was in middle school, a fact he kept quietly to himself. Each night after his mother tucked him in, the boy waited in silence for something horrifying to appear. The threat never materialized, which only served to heighten the boy's fears for the next encounter with the night. Whether it was a creature under the bed or a figure concealed in the closet, he was sure the darkness was only biding its time.

As an adult, Will no longer required a nightlight to sleep. The fantastic imagination of his childhood was no more than a forgotten memory. Unfortunately, the killer stalking them through the woods wasn't part of his imagination. The Hunter was a being of flesh and blood, one more terrifying than anything he could ever dream up. Will was once more afraid of finding himself alone in the dark.

The two men suddenly found themselves off the trail, having wandered off in the dark. Will swore out of frustration.

"What's the matter?" Cole asked.

"Nothing that couldn't be solved if you just gave me the cell phone," Will said, snarling. A glimpse of moonlight showed a path beyond the trees, and he stalked off in its direction, leaving Cole to follow.

***

Cole could feel Will starting to become unhinged, but he was powerless to do anything about it. With his leg the way it was, he was just thankful he hadn't been separated from his last remaining friend. By the time he caught up with Will, Cole was keeping his distance.

"I need time to think," Will said. "I need to remember where we are. If the storm hits before we find our way back to the lake, we'll never find our way out of here."

Cole heard the edge in Will's voice. His friend was used to being in control. Now that control had been taken from him, and they had all been rendered impotent.

I don't blame him for being afraid, Cole thought. The prospect of being lost was terrifying. Who knew what other traps the Hunter had concealed?

"Let's try raising Zack on the radio," he suggested, anxious to find out what happened to his friend.

"Suit yourself," Will said before thrusting the walkie-talkie into Cole's hand. While Will paced nervously, Cole used the opportunity to rest against a tree. His foot throbbed in constant pain.

The first time he tried to elicit a response from his friend, Cole was greeted with nothing but silence. A few minutes later, however, a voice rang out above the static.

"Cole?" It was Zack.

"Thank God it's you," Cole said, relieved. "Are you okay?" Ahead on the trail, Will stopped pacing and listened with his back turned.

"For now," Zack answered. His voice was hushed. "The killer showed up when we were talking before. He chased us through the woods. Beth and I are on our own now. Ron didn't make it."

Will returned to the spot where Cole was sitting and snatched the two-way radio out of his hands. "That's impossible," he said. "We were attacked at the same time. The valley was covered in landmines. Dave and Bart were practically blown apart."

There was a prolonged silence on the other end as Zack digested the words. Then the two men heard a female voice on the other side.

"What if there's more than one of them?"

The question hung in the air for a moment. It wasn't something any of the campers wanted to think about, but Beth's theory explained why the Hunter managed to cover so much ground effectively.

"We don't have time to worry about that right now," Will finally muttered. "It's about to start pouring rain, and when it does, Cole and I will be lost. We need to get the keys and get back to the lodge."

"I agree," Zack said. "We've gone off trail. I can see Dire Lake through the trees. We should reach Deadman's Drop in a few miles. If you come this way, be careful. When the killer passed us by, he was also headed in that direction. He might be waiting for us."

Will swore loudly. "We'll have to think about that when we get there. We were on Shatter Creek Trail headed toward the lake when we lost our way. I thought I heard an ATV and tried to find where the sound was coming from."

"It's Fields," Zack replied. "At least, it *was* Fields. We found the ATV flipped over in the mud, but no sign of Fields other than some footprints. They turned out to be a dead end."

A howl sounded in the forest behind them. Although Cole knew the animal wasn't connected to the killer, the sound still caused the hair to stand up on the back of his neck.

"We have to go," Will said, and Cole agreed. They couldn't afford to risk continuing the conversation. "Listen, you need to give us time to catch up to you. Don't leave us behind."

"I wasn't considering it," Zack said. "We'll try to get closer to the cliff, then find a place to hide and wait for you."

With that, the conversation was over.

"Do you really think he'll wait for us?" Will asked Cole.

"Why wouldn't he?"

Will stared at the ground. "I wouldn't, if we were in their shoes." His expression darkened. "It's not fair. I've always been there for Zack, haven't I? I planned this entire trip for him. It's his fault we're in this mess."

"Relax," Cole said, and Will stopped rambling. "You know Zack. He would never leave us behind."

Will didn't reply. He extended a hand and helped Cole to his feet. Cole winced as the familiar pain in his mangled limb intensified when he stood.

"We need to hurry," Will said. He shifted the shotgun to his other arm. Cole could tell the heavy gun was becoming uncomfortable to haul around.

"Do you need me to carry that for a while?"

"It's mine," Will snapped. He sighed. "I mean, with your leg the way it is, I don't think you need the extra weight on it." He handed Cole the radio instead. "Here, you can hold onto this."

It was then that Cole heard a familiar sound not far away.

"I think I hear running water," he said, hobbling through the brush.

The ground was covered in tall grasses, and their new path took them closer to the mountains. It wasn't long before they came to a creek.

"I remember this creek," Will mumbled. "It leads down from the mountains. Snowfall Creek."

"If we follow it, the creek should lead us back to the lake."

Will nodded, impressed. "Let's go," he said, and the two plotted a new course.

There was a new urgency in Will's pace Cole hadn't noticed before. As they continued, he found himself struggling more and more to keep up. His leg was bleeding worse than ever. He tried humming silently to block out the pain. The random choice of music surprised him—it was an old hymn he remembered learning in church.

Following his father's death, Cole spent several months in a fog of anger and resentment. It was one of the reasons he understood what Zack was going through. Cole eventually found solace in church. The pastor's sermons seemed to speak exactly to what troubled him, and the further involved he got in the church's youth group, the easier he found it to express the pain he was dealing with. Faith grounded him and helped shape him into the adult he would become.

Having watched friends and strangers alike die over the last few hours, Cole's faith was all that was keeping him from despair. Even so, he was starting to have doubts about his odds of survival. For not the first time that night, Cole wondered if he was going to die. He tried telling himself that if the worst happened, at least he would be reunited with his father. The thought provided little comfort.

It was cold, but not unbearably so. The landscape shifted again. Tall grasses faded away until they were on dry, patchy earth surrounded by endless rows of towering pines. The pines kept the pair largely insulated from the searing wind, though thunder continued crackling loudly above. The storm had yet to break, but Cole knew that when it did, it would be massive, untamed fury.

"This place is called the Red Pine Forest," Will said softly, as if recalling it suddenly from his memory of the map. Or perhaps it wasn't soft at all, and Will simply getting too far ahead. Without his glasses, Cole could hardly see him in the darkness.

"Will?" he called out, finally unable to distinguish between the black spot where Will had been with the other dark shapes of the forest. "Can you slow down a bit? I can't see you."

Will continued as if he hadn't heard him. When he spoke, Cole squinted and managed to discern his friend's outline moving under the trees.

"We're getting closer to the lake," Will said, almost to himself. "If we go through the forest instead of moving along the creek, we can cut the distance in half."

Cole followed silently, not that he had much of a choice. He felt a chill run down his spine when they left the creek behind. Compounded by his distorted vision, the expansive forest, twisted in the darkness and moonlight, looked monstrous in its own right. The tall and narrow trees looked down at them, adorned in thornlike leafy projections. Cole felt like the trees, or perhaps something else, was watching him.

He was so busy looking at the trees, he didn't see the pinecone resting deceptively on the barren soil. Cole stepped on it with his wounded foot. This time, he cried out in pain. Cole sank to the ground.

Will turned around, his face etched in anger. "Are you crazy? Zack *just* said the killer was headed in the direction of the lake. Do you want him to hear us?"

Cole mumbled an apology through gritted teeth. There were tears in his eyes from the pain.

"We don't have time for this," Will said. "Pick yourself up and come on."

As Cole started to rise, he could swear he saw a shape move in the darkness not too far away. Without his glasses, he had no way to be sure. The terrain turned downward, and he followed Will down a slope. This time, he heard the footsteps behind them.

Cole quickened his pace until he caught up with Will. He quietly tugged on his friend's shirt.

"Someone is following us," he whispered. He felt Will's body tense.

***

Will cast a glance over his shoulder at the hill from which they had just descended. Standing under the full light of the moon, the killer stared down at them.

Snarling, Will brought the shotgun up and pulled the trigger without bothering to aim the weapon. The murderer simply stood in place, watching as the bullet cleared the trees nowhere near him. In response, the killer withdrew a handgun and fired at him. The bullet tore through the tree next to Will. Panicking, Will turned and ran. He was exposed in the moonlight, and the Hunter was a much better shot than he was.

I have to find a place to hide, Will thought desperately.

"Will!" Cole shouted, grabbing his arm. "You're going too fast!"

Another bullet passed over Will's head. The killer was toying with them. Will grappled with Cole, looking nervously at the trees. The Hunter had vanished from sight. Wherever he was, the killer was too close. Will knew he wouldn't be able to defend himself with the shotgun unless the Hunter came close enough that accuracy didn't matter. The Hunter would find them and kill them, just like the others.

In the spur of the moment, a new thought occurred to Will. Tightening his grip on Cole, he reached down into his friend's pants pocket and wrenched the cell phone free. Before Cole could react, he grabbed him and threw him against the ground.

"What are you doing?" Cole shouted as he fell.

Will looked down at his friend for a moment before running as fast as his legs could take him.

"Will!"

He heard Cole's voice carrying over the trees. Will blocked the voice out and focused on the darkness ahead as he abandoned the pines for the thicker forest to the north, using the cell phone's light to guide him. Once he was close enough to the lodge, he would use the phone to call for help. If Cole remained alive, the police would return to the pines and rescue him. In the back of his mind, Will knew this was unlikely. Abandoning Cole to the Hunter meant ensuring his own survival, since Will now had enough time to escape himself. That was all that mattered. He tore through the brush, holding onto the knowledge he would do whatever it took to survive.

***

"Will!" Cole shouted again. His voice broke. He stumbled forward, feeling out with his hands. Dark clouds now covered the sky, concealing the faint moonlight. Darkness reigned again. Cole whispered his friend's name a final time out of despair. He was alone. The killer was probably somewhere nearby.

Behind him, he heard a pinecone crunch under the Hunter's weight. Sucking in a deep breath of air, Cole charged through the forest at full speed, reeling from the pain of his injury. He stumbled over a rock in the blackness and picked himself up, glancing behind to see if he was being pursued. Though he couldn't see anything following him, the feeling of being watched persisted, so Cole kept running. Ahead, the clouds lifted and the moonlight returned. The wind howled and he heard what sounded like whispers in the forest.

Just as he was about to leave the pines behind, the earth opened under his feet, and Cole plunged into darkness.

CHAPTER FOURTEEN

2:47 AM

SWEEPING WINDS RATTLED THE CABIN door on its hinges. The door shook violently, and the floorboards creaked inside the long-abandoned structure. On the second floor, the occupant concealed inside the closet stirred.

It was still dark when Dave awoke. His eyes opened slowly, resisting a return to the nightmarish reality that engulfed him. The light of the full moon, which glowed so brightly through the cabin windows a few hours ago, had disappeared from sight. Dave felt around as he attempted to regain his bearings. His entire body ached. When he gently reached to his back and ran a hand down his side, Dave felt a stinging sensation in his shoulder. The wound hadn't even begun to heal.

What time is it? he wondered. It was still night. That much was certain. Dave swore quietly, angry with himself for falling asleep. The others might have tried to contact him. Maybe they succeeded in finding help. He would never know. Dave rose from the ground to get a better view through the closet's shutters. There was a sticky mess on the floorboards beneath him. It was a dried pool of his blood. As he fell backwards, his hand brushed against the two-way radio. Dave remembered switching it off. He cradled the radio in his hands like it offered him protection from being alone. Even sitting in the dark, concealed within the shadowy confines of the cabin, he felt exposed.

His throat was parched. Mustering his courage, Dave pushed open the twin closet doors and crawled back into the desolate room next to the staircase. The house was unnaturally quiet. He approached the window, aware of the faint echo of thunder coming from outside. The cold floor gave him chills. Dave peered through the window at the forest below. The tall trees that grew on the mountainside swayed about in the harsh wind. A sea of clouds partially obscured the moon, evidence of an impending storm.

The sound of thunder vanished, replaced by the noise of the door rattling below. The noise unnerved Dave. He kept expecting to see a figure emerge from the dark forest and make its way to the cabin. Dave forced himself to pull his gaze away from the window.

I need to find a bathroom, he thought, suddenly aware his bladder was full. He wanted to wash the bloodstains off his skin. If he had the strength afterward, he would wander downstairs and see if there was a first aid kit anywhere in sight. Based on the way things were going, he doubted it.

The bathroom was a modest room directly in front of the staircase. On its left was the second bedroom on the top floor. Dave was grateful he didn't have to crawl down the stairs to reach the restroom. Grabbing the countertop, he pulled himself up and tried flicking on the light-switch. It didn't work. With fumbling hands, Dave turned on the faucet instead. Thankfully, rushing water erupted into the sink. He splashed his face with water and gazed at the mirror. Although obscured by darkness, his reflection looked bad. It was like he was staring at another person.

"I was shot," Dave muttered, trying to convince himself it really happened as he gulped down water directly from the spout.

Downstairs, the doorknob of the front door began to shake. Dave's eyes grew wide. He couldn't remember locking, or even closing, the door behind him after he forced his way inside earlier.

In a panic, he turned off the water and dropped to the floor. As Dave crawled back into the hall, he heard the front door swing open on the first floor. He prayed it was just the wind, and listened for any sound in the silent house.

The floorboards rattled under the weight of the intruder, and Dave realized he wasn't alone. Someone was with him inside the cabin. Moving as quietly as he could, Dave crawled toward the bedroom where he had hid before. He peeked through the balcony posts to catch a glimpse of the intruder, but all he saw was a shadow. The intruder took two more steps. Rather than wait for the stranger to come looking for him, Dave decided to keep moving. His heart was pounding. If he made a loud noise, he was done for. He now regretted being so quick to strike out on his own.

Miraculously, the intruder appeared to walk into one of the bedrooms on the first floor. Using the chance to hide, Dave slid into the closet on his belly. Suddenly, the floor creaked under him. He heard the footsteps stop below. The intruder had heard the sound. The stranger's footsteps started again, and this time they grew louder and louder until Dave heard him coming up the stairs. Dave pulled the closet doors closed and prayed it was too dark for the intruder to see him.

He switched on the two-way radio. His hands shaking, Dave held it up to his mouth.

"Guys?" he whispered into the receiver. "I'm in one of the cabins. Someone is in here with me."

The only response was the sound of static. No one was coming to his rescue. For all he knew, his friends had already made it to safety.

The cabin, which had been his greatest hope to wait out the attack until morning, was now a trap he was snared in. How had the killer found him? Dave was sure no one followed him through the forest. Was the Hunter toying with them the whole time?

The killer reached the top of the stairs. From his vantage point in the closet, Dave still couldn't see where the man was. He heard the intruder shuffling down the hallway, and then Dave heard a water droplet fall from the faucet in the bathroom. The footsteps drew closer.

Maybe he'll think it's a leak, Dave thought.

The intruder walked into the bedroom. Sweat dripped down Dave's face. The man walked over to the window, and Dave could see him through the closet shutters. He could barely see the killer in the darkness. A bandana masked his face. Dave watched the killer stare out the window before turning and moving toward the bed. The intruder dropped to his knees and reached under the bed. Dave's breathing accelerated. Maybe the killer would pass him by.

The killer stood and walked in the direction of the closet. He was looking directly above Dave. A second water droplet fell in the bathroom. At the sound, the killer turned and walked out of the room. Dave watched the man's black boots vanish from sight. When the Hunter was gone, he let out a quiet sigh of relief. Dave thought he heard the sound of the man's footsteps going down the stairs. He waited several minutes and crawled out of the closet. He wanted to get to the window to see if the intruder was gone. Dave crouched by the windowsill and peeked outside. There was nothing below. The door remained open, swaying in the breeze.

Where did he go?

Across the hall, the door to the second bedroom opened silently. A shadowy figure appeared in the doorway behind Dave, who was busy staring out the window. By the time Dave heard the man's footsteps, the intruder was almost on top of him. He turned around and saw the man creeping toward him. Dave stumbled and fell back, landing on the floor. The killer reached out and seized his leg, raising a hunting knife with his other hand.

Fighting with all he had left, Dave kicked as hard as he could. The kick caught the killer by surprise, and the man crashed against the wall. Dave pushed himself to his feet and hobbled out of the room. The masked man was right behind him. The killer struck Dave in the back, and he tumbled down the wooden stairs. Dave hit the ground below hard. He could taste blood. His world was spinning.

The killer slowly descended the stairs. Dave tried to rise, and faltered as he crawled toward the open front door. Floorboards creaked again behind him. He looked back and saw the killer towering at his back, knife in hand.

The blade plunged into his back again. Dave sank closer to the ground, a silent scream on his lips. The door loomed mere feet away. Finding a final reserve of strength, he inched a hand closer to the opening and pulled himself toward it.

The killer stepped on his hand with a boot, pinning him to the ground. Dave tried to struggle, but the intruder pulled his blade free and he stabbed him again and again. This time the weapon finished its task.

***

When his work was done, Rodney Crowe departed the cabin and headed into the wind. They all thought they could hide. How wrong they were. The Hunter taught him that. Of the two of them, there was no doubt who was the more experienced. The Hunter started playing the game long before Crowe came along. Exactly how long, Crowe couldn't say. He didn't even know the man's real name. It didn't matter. They were kindred spirits. Crowe had been a murderer many times over before crossing paths with the Hunter, but the man taught him things he'd never dreamt of.

There were differences between them. Crowe reveled in the act of murder itself. The Hunter enjoyed the game more. The Hunter also took pleasure from toying with his victims, watching them fracture physically and emotionally. There was also that necklace of his. The Hunter's fixation on the item didn't bother Crowe initially, but that was starting to change. Crowe even caught the other man talking to it earlier when his friend thought he didn't see. He was starting to suspect the Hunter had a secret motive for the killings other than his own amusement.

Crowe pushed the suspicions from his mind. There would be another time to dwell on the state of their partnership. That time wasn't during the game, not when he had a real shot at winning. Soon there would be a reckoning, but for now it was time the rest of the campers shared a reunion of their own.

The final phase of the game was about to begin.

***

Whispering Reach towered above, beckoning like a siren over the black waters of Dire Lake. Dark clouds covered the sky, all but masking the moon. The wind ripped through the trees with powerful force, which caused the smaller saplings to bend and snap. A few drops of rain fell from the sky, a sign the heavens were about to open.

"How much longer are we going to wait?"

It was a fair question. At the moment, Zack didn't know how to answer. He looked Beth over carefully, watching her in what remained of the moonlight. Fear was still visible on her face. Determination was there too. She wanted to survive. When Lily died, Zack had lost his zeal for life. How did Beth continue to function given the death of her companion? Zack wondered how long she and Ron were dating before the camping trip. He didn't see a ring on her finger, so it was obvious they were not yet married.

"They're coming. I know it."

In reality, he knew no such thing. Cole and Will were both skilled hikers, but the killer's game had flipped convention onto its head. Nevertheless, Beth seemed to believe him when he told her they would pull through.

The pair hid in the brush, less than a mile from the cliff. Deadman's Drop loomed not far away. Zack picked their hiding place well. A well-kempt path to the east was called the Endless Trail, which supposedly led from one end of the park to the other. Following this trail would also take them back to the park entrance. If push came to shove, they could take the second route and avoid making the climb up the cliff in the rain.

"Tell me about her."

"Who?"

"The woman you lost."

Zack couldn't recall if he'd mentioned anything about the person he'd lost being a woman, but Beth watched him with a knowing gleam in her eye. He sat in silence for a moment, fiddling with the flashlight. Lily's death wasn't something he could just start talking about, even with Cole. At the same time, when would be the right time to talk about it? If not now, he might never have the chance.

"Her name was Lily. She took her life." Other than blinking, Beth remained motionless. It seemed insane to be having such a conversation at a time like this, but now that he'd started, Zack found he couldn't stop. "She'd cheated on me, so I pushed her away when she tried to reach out for help. I just couldn't see her pain. Or maybe I chose to ignore it."

Beth didn't reply. She didn't try to tell him Lily's death wasn't his fault. She didn't ask him any further questions. She just listened. When Zack finished, they both sat quietly in the shadows of the trees that helped conceal them, listening to the sound of the wind.

A few minutes later, Zack realized that someone was moving toward the lake from the south, and fast. The hair bristled on Zack's arms. He stood quickly.

"Be ready to run," he whispered to Beth. A shape took form in the distance, blurred from the speed with which it was moving. As it drew nearer, Zack spotted a shotgun in the figure's hands. Beth's mouth dropped in horror.

The figure spotted them. With impossible speed, the shape

changed course and headed for them, leaving trampled bushes and broken branches in his wake.

Zack's entire body experienced a cold chill that ran through him like a wave. He felt the color drain from his cheeks. "Run!" he started to shout.

It was too late. The figure was within shooting range. Before either Zack or Beth could flee from their current position, the shape cleared a fallen log and raised his gun in their direction.

Thinking quickly, Zack switched on the flashlight and shone it in the intruder's eyes. At the same time, Beth clubbed the blinded figure over the head with a large rock. The man tumbled to the ground with a short cry of pain.

It was then that Zack recognized the person illuminated by the flashlight.

"Will?" he muttered, shocked.

His friend stared back at him with squinted eyes. There was a strange expression on his face, almost empty, yet feral in some way. Will's sweat-covered clothes were torn, and his arms and face were masked in abrasions from branches and thorns. He panted heavily and tried to rise while leaning against a tree.

Zack switched off the flashlight. "Sorry about that."

Beth continued watching Will with a steel expression, and Zack wondered what occurred between them when the two met earlier that day. Will alluded to it before the campers retired for the night, but there was suspicion in her eyes that troubled Zack.

"It's okay," Zack said to reassure her. "He's with us."

Will stumbled, and Zack helped steady him.

"That blow to the head threw me off balance," he said. He bent over and picked up the shotgun. "You're lucky I didn't shoot you both on accident."

Zack almost smiled. After being separated from his friends for so long, it was good to see one of them again. For a while, he thought it would never happen.

Suddenly, he realized who was missing.

"Wait a second," Zack said, his voice filled with dread. "Where's Cole?"

Will's left hand unconsciously reached toward his back pocket. "I'm so sorry, Zack. He didn't make it." The thunder echoed above, and more tiny raindrops spilled out of the sky.

Zack swallowed. He closed his eyes for a moment, overcome by utter exhaustion.

"What happened?" His voice was flat. None of the others had deserved their fates, Cole least of all. It wasn't fair.

"The killer got him. I barely got away."

"I'm sorry, Zack," Beth said. She rested a hand on his back.

"Then we're the last ones," Zack said. "Everyone else is dead."

"It's not over yet," said Beth.

Will nodded. "The killer said he'd give us until dawn. If we can stay alive a few more hours and outlast him, we can make it out of this. It's what Cole would have wanted," he added for good measure.

"You're right," Zack said. "Are we still going to make for the cliff?" He gestured past the trees, where Deadman's Drop waited amidst the impending storm. Beth and Will nodded. "Then let's go." Zack started to emerge from the forest, but Will grabbed him.

"Wait," Will said. "If the killer sees us on the cliff and we're all up there, we'll all be trapped."

Zack frowned. "What are you suggesting?"

"There's no reason for all of us to die," Will whispered. "Two of us should take the Endless Trail and find the long way back to the lodge. The other person should grab the keys and meet us there." Zack noticed the use of the word *us*. "Obviously it shouldn't be her," Will continued, pointing at Beth. "We're the only ones who know where to look for the keys. And we have more experience."

Zack's frown deepened. "I'm not sure I like the idea of splitting up again." Not after he'd worked so hard to find his friends.

"Neither do I, but we don't have a choice," Will said.

"I agree," Beth added. She looked at Zack. "You and I will make it back to the lodge and wait for your friend to join us."

Will shook his head. "It can't be that way. Zack is the better climber. Besides, I've hurt my leg. And that bump on my head has left me shaky. With a climb that steep, we can't risk it. It has to be Zack."

Your leg didn't seem to be injured when you were running toward us earlier, Zack thought. Still, if Will wanted to take the coward's way out, so be it.

"Fine," he said. He would do what needed to be done for the group. "Give me your word you'll keep Beth safe."

"Of course," Will said, like it was the most natural thing in the world. He even attempted a smile. "She's in safe hands with me."

Zack started to leave again.

"Wait," Beth said. "Shouldn't Zack have the gun, if he's going up there alone?"

Fear flashed in Will's eyes. "He won't be up there long," he stammered. "It'll be harder to make his way up the cliff while holding the gun. Besides, I'll need it to protect you."

The last point hit home with Zack.

"Agreed," he whispered. "You two stay safe." He grabbed Beth's hand and gave it a squeeze. "You're going to make it out of this."

He just wished he believed it.

CHAPTER FIFTEEN

3:23 AM

THE HEAVENS OPENED, UNSHACKLING THE deluge that had slowly built over the course of the night. Thunder rumbled across Drifter's Folly as faint echoes of lightning illuminated random scenes of horror strung throughout the park. Heavy drops of rain poured and poured with no apparent end in sight.

To the man climbing the dangerous trail known as Deadman's Drop, the rain was a simultaneous source of danger and protection. While it was true the killer would likely find it harder to track him in the dark, wetness made the incline leading to the cliff's peak even more treacherous than usual. Without the light of the moon to guide him, Zack was faced with no option but to keep going forward. He used the flashlight when he dared, knowing full well it risked exposing his presence to any onlookers.

Zack wondered briefly if any campers other than Will and Beth remained alive in the park. There was always the possibility Ranger Fields was alive, since Zack had never seen the man's corpse. Even so, he knew better than to count on Fields showing up to save the day. Instead, it fell to Zack to retrieve the keys to the van. Zack grabbed the trunk of a small tree and pulled himself forward, almost slipping on a wet rock in the process. He collapsed under the tree to catch his breath.

He was soaked to the bone. Zack reached into his pocket for the flashlight. He shone the beam into the darkness below, turned the light off, and waited for a response. For a moment, there was nothing other than the pitter-pattering of the rain. A few seconds later, he saw Beth's light coming from the trees. She and Will had seen his signal, and they had started on their way down the Endless Trail. Returning the flashlight to his pocket, Zack climbed to his feet. The storm thundered on, ignoring the man slowly making his way up the steep cliff.

It wasn't long before he almost slipped again. He remembered falling on his way down Deadman's Drop as his friends tore down the trail to escape the killer hours ago. He was lucky he hadn't broken his neck then and there. He survived that, and he promised himself he would survive this. Getting his friends out of this mess gave him a purpose, a reason to live. He promised Ron he would keep Beth alive, and he didn't intend to break his word—even if that meant putting himself in danger. Zack didn't have to be a mind reader to see the worry in Beth's eyes when Will paired himself with her. He wasn't blind. A troubling change had taken place in his friend. Unfortunately, he was out of options. If anyone could reach the top of Whispering Reach in this weather, it was Zack.

That the majestic splendor of the park hours earlier had morphed into the terrifying landscape surrounding him now wasn't lost on Zack. Higher and higher he climbed, occasionally stopping to signal to the pair below or to regain his bearings. Eventually he neared the top of the trail. The peak was in sight, and he could just see the tip of the tent from the trail. Zack slowed his pace. Lightning flashed around him, piercing the blackness with eerie light. Most of the park was visible from the cliff. Zack could see the recreation area, the rivers flowing into the lake, and even the trail leading to the cemetery he'd stumbled across earlier.

The rainfall wasn't quite as heavy atop Whispering Reach, and Zack could see several breaks in the storm from the cliff. A prolonged bout of thunder told him not to mistake the temporary lull for a sign the storm had reached its end. He scanned the landscape below for any sign of movement. Other than the trees swaying in the wind, there was none to be found. Zack shone his light at the trees below, flicking it off and on twice to let the others know that he'd reached the top. He took in a deep breath, stepped off the trail, and onto the peak.

The campsite appeared largely the same as they left it. The back of the tent, which remained partially unzipped, flapped harshly to and fro in the wind. In contrast, the front of the tent stood largely still, as if beckoning him inward. The fire had long since died away. The rain quickly extinguished any embers that endured.

Zack felt a chill run down his spine. There was an eerie feeling in returning to the place where one of his friends had been murdered only hours ago. This was where it all started. Zack hoped this was where the nightmare would end. The edge of the forest lay several feet from the tent, shrouded in darkness in the absence of moonlight. After pausing for a moment, Zack took a few steps forward. The skin crawled on the back of his neck. Like before, he couldn't shake the feeling something was wrong. He looked from side to side, searching for something out of place. When no deranged figure appeared under the trees, he figured he was alone.

Lightning flashed, and he saw a trail of blood leading from the tent. As darkness returned, Zack switched on the flashlight. Its beam flickered, growing dim.

"Not now," he muttered, tapping it against his leg. The light grew strong again. Using the light, he followed the trail of blood until he saw something resting in the dirt beyond the tent. Even in the shadows, he could tell it was a human body.

Steve, he realized. The corpse unsettled him. After shooting him, the killer had dragged Steve out of the tent and did God-knew-what with him. Or perhaps Steve stumbled out of the tent all on his own, looking for the friends who abandoned him in the few seconds of life he had left. Zack quickly switched the light off and looked away in disgust.

I promise you, the man who did this will pay, Zack thought. He and the others would survive this and alert the police, but first he needed the keys. Zack turned away from the body and sprinted toward the tent. He hesitated at the entrance before being swallowed by the darkness as he stepped inside. He switched the flashlight back on. According to Will, the keys to the van were inside his pack. He found the pack next to his friend's sleeping bag. Thrusting shaking hands inside the bag, he looked for the keys in the pack's front pouch.

It was empty.

The flashlight flickered and went out. This time, the light didn't return when he shook the flashlight. Zack swore as he grappled in the lightless tent. He tore through the rest of the pack and felt blindly for the keys. They were nowhere to be found. A wave of panic rose within him.

Lightning flashed over Whispering Reach, illuminating the body outside the tent. As Zack scrambled to find the keys, he didn't see the body start to move. The figure rose silently, unnoticed by the camper amid the darkness. The rain drowned out all noise outside the tent. As he slid forward like a ghost, the shadow reached into a holster and took out a jagged hunting knife.

"Come on," Zack whispered angrily. He dropped to the ground and fumbled around in the dark. If the keys weren't in the pack, then where were they?

Zack bumped into something large under one of the blankets. He pulled the sheet back just as the lightning flashed again. In the white light he could see Steve's pale face, forever frozen in horror. His heart had been cut out.

A horrifying realization dawned on him.

If that's Steve, then whose body was outside the tent?

He looked back at the exact moment the killer came at him

with the knife. Zack kicked back desperately. The killer stumbled backward against the side of the tent. As Zack tried to crawl out the back of the tent, the killer recovered and grabbed his leg.

"Get back here," Crowe said, pouncing onto him. Zack pushed against the killer's strength, lost his balance, and the two fell to the ground. The killer had him pinned. Unmasked, the killer's face was every bit as savage as Zack had imagined. Only the eyes were wrong somehow. Before, the Hunter's eyes had been black. This man's eyes were green.

"You're the tiebreaker," Crowe whispered as he struggled to bury the knife into the man beneath him. Zack fought back with a strength that surprised him, but his energy was fleeting. The knife inched closer and closer to the camper's face.

Zack reached out blindly with his free hand, trying to grab anything in the darkness. His hand found the dead flashlight, and he brought it up hard against the killer's head. The move shifted the balance of the struggle enough for Zack to push himself free. Lightning flashed, and the two men stood facing each other in the tent. The killer grinned, still holding the knife. He was taunting him. Zack bumped against the supply kit and silently reached inside. His hand closed around a screwdriver.

"I'm going to enjoy this," Crowe said, advancing with the knife.

Instead of trying to run, Zack charged him holding the screwdriver. Crowe lashed out with the knife, but he wasn't fast enough. As he cut through the man's flesh with the knife, he felt searing pain.

Zack heard the killer scream when he jammed the screwdriver into his eye. The instrument didn't penetrate far enough to kill the murderer, though it put out the eye. Zack didn't have time to gloat. He could feel himself bleeding where the killer's knife had cut him across the chest. Zack blocked out the pain and stumbled out of the tent. He started toward the forest when he saw something glowing on the ground in the moonlight.

The keys! Steve must have grabbed them when he was trying to escape. Zack turned back and scooped up the keys. Thunder rolled loudly above. The killer stood just outside the tent. He ripped the screwdriver out and unleashed a scream laden with rage. The killer stood between Zack and the forest. There was no going back down Deadman's Drop.

Crowe lifted a gun into the air.

Zack took a few steps back. His shoes slid over the wet ground. He cast a glance behind him. He was pushed to the edge of Whispering Reach. Dire Lake rested behind him. Certain death lay ahead. Zack pivoted, wheeled around, and began sprinting for the edge.

The killer pulled the trigger.

Zack stumbled as the first bullet ripped into him, but managed to keep going. He reached the end of the cliff and jumped as the killer pulled the trigger again.

"Lily," Zack whispered as he fell, pelted by rain. He closed his eyes and let the water wash over him.

In the sky, the clouds once again swallowed the moon.

***

The storm passed over Red Pine Forest, leaving almost total silence in its wake. Torrents of rain turned to droplets before finally fading to a light mist. Only the darkness remained. As the wind died down, a few pine needles fluttered down into a deep hole dug into the earth. Once cleverly masked by brush and branches, the pit was now exposed.

One of the pine needles landed gently on the man sprawled out at the bottom of the hole. The man moaned, awakening to pain and blackness. Cole's eyes snapped open. It took several moments for him to be able to think clearly amid the aching of his body.

Where am I? he wondered, grappling about in the mud. He could no longer feel his injured foot at all. Cole blindly pressed against a dirt wall with his left hand in an attempt to find the edge. The wall continued upwards indefinitely. As he pushed himself against the wall, Cole attempted to stand. He screamed as soon as he tried moving his legs. Cole slid and sank into the mud. His breath came out in short, labored gasps. Cole gingerly brought his hand to his chest. Several of his ribs felt broken.

He remained still for several moments until some of the pain slowly abated. His eyes adjusted to the darkness, and he began to put together what had happened. Seeing the intruder in the tent, stepping on the bear trap, being abandoned by Will—all of it. The last thing he remembered was the ground opening beneath his feet.

It was yet another of the traps in the forest, just like the landmines or the bear trap. Without his glasses, Cole had run right into it. He reached out cautiously to feel his surroundings. His right hand had difficulty responding to his thoughts. It too felt broken, and Cole could feel dislocated bone protruding through his skin. A wave of nausea welled inside him.

Cole shivered. His clothes were soaking wet, probably from a mixture of the rain and the small pool of water filling the hole. He was covered in mud. The smell of the water seemed like gasoline to him, but in his haze he wasn't sure why.

How long was I out? Cole wondered. The Hunter was almost upon them when Will had abandoned him. Cole prayed he'd managed to put enough distance between himself and the Hunter before falling into the hole. As it was, he wasn't going anywhere anytime soon.

He tried removing his cell phone from his pocket before remembering that Will had stolen it. The night's chaos had exposed an inner savagery in Will that Cole had always suspected was there, though Zack was always blind to it. In the midst of his desperation, a thought suddenly struck him. What about the two-way radio? Cole reached into his other pants pocket. He froze as his hands once again grasped empty space. It was gone.

Cole wasn't ready to die. He had too much to do in life. Besides, Zack needed him, especially if Will was as far gone as Cole believed. A man who would do whatever it took to survive was someone who was extremely dangerous. Cole needed to get out of the hole. He had to find some way to warn his friend.

As the clouds continued their retreat across the sky, moonlight spilled into the pit. Cole looked up in despair. The way out was so close, yet so far away at the same time. Even if the slick wall was climbable, his body was too mangled to attempt the feat.

That was when he spotted the two-way radio. It loomed at the opposite end of the pit, just above the pool of water covering the base of the hole. It must have fallen out when he fell. Praying the device was still functional, Cole tried to reposition himself so that he could attempt to reach it. He winced. Even the slightest movement brought searing pain. This was going to take some time.

A loud cracking noise echoed above the wind, which had died down to a faint whisper. The sound made his blood run cold. He could hear distinct footsteps growing closer. They grew louder with each second that passed.

"Guys?" he called into the night, hoping against hope his friends had found him.

The footsteps stopped. No one answered. In that moment, Cole knew the killer had come for him. The how or why no longer mattered—all that mattered was warning the others. Eyeing the two-way radio, he made a desperate effort to reach the device. He crawled forward in the mud, moving through the pain. Each inch brought new levels of agony.

The footsteps started again. Cole was aware he was being watched. Tapping his last reserve of strength, he stretched his body out and pushed toward the end of the hole. A shadowy figure appeared above and blocked the moonlight from streaming into the hole. Cole reached out, grasping for the antenna. He felt the fingers of his right hand touch the end of the device.

It slipped out of his grip. It was over. Cole braced himself for bullets that never came. When he looked up, the figure was gone. Gritting his teeth, Cole seized the opportunity and dragged himself forward a few more inches. This time, he grabbed the two-way radio and clutched it tightly in his hands. He was overcome with relief.

A twig snapped above, and Cole's eyes widened in fear. The killer had been watching the entire time, waiting to see if he would reach the radio. Cole stared up at the killer, who bore into him with black eyes that seemed to shine in the night. The man reached into his pocket and took out a small object. Cole squinted, trying to see what he was doing.

The Hunter lit a match and held it gently in his fingers, examining the flame.

Cole pressed the call button on the radio, desperately trying to reach his friends. He heard what sounded like a voice masked by static on the other end.

The Hunter dropped the match into the hole.

As the light was descending, it finally dawned on Cole why the pool of water in the hole smelled like gasoline. He didn't have time to think anything else. His body erupted into flame. His finger still on the call button, with his last breath he uttered an unearthly scream.

***

The killer watched the man inside the hole burn until the fire died away, then turned and vanished into the darkness.

Now there were only three left.

CHAPTER SIXTEEN

4:06 AM

Z ACK'S BODY SANK, SUSPENDED IN a void. In the water, there was only blackness. A stream of bubbles flooded from his mouth, diminishing with each second that passed after he'd struck the surface. The sea of water threatened to become his tomb.

"Zack," a voice whispered softly. It was then that he opened his eyes.

Looming menacingly above Dire Lake, the sky was as dark as it had been all night. Raindrops mingled with the black waters of the lake, creating an ever-shifting collage of ripples. Small waves gently rocked a splintered canoe tied to the dock with frayed rope, bashing it against the faded wood. Thunder roared across the park, as if threatening to shake the very foundations of the cliff towering above.

Zack's hand tore free of the water. Moments later, his head surged above the waves. He gasped for air before vanishing back into the depths below. A few seconds passed before he emerged from the shallow waters at the edge of the lake, clenching the muddy shore.

Zack sucked in a lungful of air and collapsed onto the shore. The thick mud felt soothing against his aching body. Lightning flashed temporarily, revealing blood mingled with the mud.

He felt a sharp pain in his right arm, close to the shoulder. From what he could tell, the bullet had only grazed him. He was lucky. A fall from that height could have easily ended the killer's work if he had landed in the wrong place.

Zack rested atop the wet shore as long as he dared until he mustered the will to rise. He sensed a presence watching him when he was in the water. It was somehow different than before, when he'd felt the killer's eyes on him in the darkness. Zack rolled over and pushed himself up. The Hunter would be coming for him now. Of that, he was sure. Zack remembered the look of rage in the killer's face when he pulled the screwdriver out of his eye socket. The killer was probably already well on his way down Deadman's Drop to make sure Zack was dead.

Lighting flashed again, and he saw a figure staring down at him from Whispering Reach. Zack swore and stumbled toward the forest. He had enough of a head start to find a place to hide before the killer caught up with him. At the edge of the forest, Zack's foot caught on a rock and he landed on the ground. He cast a quick look behind him. The shadow on the edge of Whispering Reach was gone.

Where do I go? Zack thought. No matter where they turned, the Hunter was always right around the corner. There was no way out. Zack struggled to recognize the dark recesses of the forest, but everything seemed foreign to him in the blackness and the storm. Above him, the heavy rain easily penetrated the cover provided by the trees. Harsh winds chilled him straight to the bone through his soaked clothes. He could feel blood continuing to trickle from the shallow wound close to his shoulder.

Nothing looked familiar. Besides, he was so tired. Tired of running. Tired of fighting to survive. Zack knew he was moving too slowly, but he was powerless to do anything about it. His body was exhausted. If he didn't find a place to crash soon, he would lose consciousness in the forest. Zack stumbled and grabbed a wide tree to steady himself. Though faint slivers of moonlight now shone through the trees, he could hardly see anything through the torrential rain.

He kept running, minute after minute. It felt like hours. His legs turned to lead. Zack's body started to betray him. His heart was pounding. He fell forward onto the ground. This was the end. Zack didn't know what made him look up as his eyes started to close. Whatever the reason, it was then he spotted the entrance to the cave. Suddenly, he remembered walking into the cave hours earlier with Cole. The memory felt like a lifetime ago.

"Shallow Water Cave," he mumbled, his voice drowned out by the storm. Zack found the strength to rise one last time. Before he lumbered into the cave, he tried disguising his tracks. Though damp and dark, the cave proved far drier than the storm. Zack remembered telling Beth that hiding in a cave was to be avoided unless there was no other choice. As things stood, he was out of choices.

Zack reached into his pocket, searching for the keys to the van. They were gone. He must have lost them when he plunged into the lake. Will and Beth would have to find another way out of the park. Despite the Hunter's promise that safety waited for those who could escape the boundaries of the park, Zack suspected getting out of Drifter's Folly wasn't going to prove that easy. While failing to find the keys, Zack did find another item in his left pocket: the two-way radio. Maybe he could contact the others yet.

The radio was completely drenched. Zack tried turning it on. Nothing happened. This didn't surprise Zack, who doubted the device was waterproof. Now he had no way of knowing what happened to Beth and Will. He hoped the killer hadn't caught up with them first. The prospect of being the only person left alive in the entire park terrified him.

Maybe if the killer comes after me, they can reach the lodge, he thought. *Maybe it's for the best.* The killer would likely find him in the end, but not before the other two escaped. After enduring the last months with no reason to keep going, he only had to push a little harder to keep his friends safe, and then he could let go.

Zack wandered farther into the cave. He was reluctant to venture too far inside, with no way to see what waited for him, but he also feared not going far enough in case the killer was still on his trail. After realizing he was still holding the dead two-way radio, he let the device tumble to the earth beneath his feet. He wandered a little farther until he was overcome by the need to rest. He found a place to hide on the other side of a large rock formation and eased himself to the ground. Zack closed his eyes and slept.

***

There was nothing there. Austin Fields swore loudly. The park ranger returned his pistol to its holster. There was no mistaking the sound of gunshots he'd heard almost twenty minutes ago. He followed the sound to the lake, hoping to run into any of the remaining campers. They were playing on the Hunter's ground now, and Fields doubted they truly understood the magnitude of that.

He thought he heard a twig snap, although it was impossible to tell in the rain.

"Hello?" he called. He silently slid his hand toward his holster. "Is anyone there?" No one answered. He was alone.

But he wasn't alone, was he? There were others in the forest. He needed to find the campers first, before they ran into anyone else. Fields had hoped some of them would stumble across the ATV he'd overturned deeper in the forest. Surely they had heard it. Maybe they had heard the ATV, only they were unable to make their way to it. Drifter's Folly was covered in traps, as Fields knew well.

He'd seen the bodies. The more people who died, the harder it grew to find the remaining survivors. That's what happened when someone thinned the herd.

He withdrew to the relative cover provided by the trees and moved farther away from Whispering Reach. He could see several broken branches and uprooted weeds in a clearing not far from a wide trail nearby. Fields dropped to a knee and took out a flashlight. The tracks were clear. There were two pairs, moving together down the Endless Trail. It was a path that would take them toward the entrance to Drifter's Folly.

They would never reach it in time.

Fields switched off the light and started making his way down the trail. He needed to catch up to them before anyone else did.

***

"You have to wake up."

Everything was light. It was so bright he could barely see. The contrast with the monstrous storm raging over Drifter's Folly couldn't have been sharper.

Her voice spoke again, this time with an added urgency.

"You have to wake up." He'd know that voice anywhere. It was the one that had haunted his dreams—it was *her* voice.

"Lily?" He wasn't sure if this was real or if he was hallucinating, but this was no flashback.

"Don't let him win, Zack."

The killer's footsteps echoed in the cave.

Moonlight spilled into the entrance, revealing the man's shadow moving along the wall. Still on the floor, Zack crawled backward while following the intruder with his eyes. He could feel the wet fabric of his pants scraping against the rock. He pushed himself against a wall and waited. Zack caught a glimpse of the killer's bow a few minutes later through a hole in the rock formation in front of him. The killer materialized soon after, advancing slowly through the cave. He was wearing some kind of goggles on his head, which Zack guessed allowed him to see in the dark.

How did he find me? Zack wondered. He had tried to cover his tracks. Zack tried not to panic, but the killer was getting closer.

With the goggles, the man would spot him easily. There was no way out. Zack slid backward a little farther and his hand brushed across something wet. A pair of dead eyes greeted him when he peered into the darkness, where a bloated corpse floated in a pool of water. It was all he could do not to scream. He managed to stifle the sound before drawing the attention of his pursuer. As his eyes continued to adjust to the dark, he paused to inspect the body.

Zack didn't recognize the remains. This didn't surprise him; however long the corpse had been rotting in the cave, it could only be considered human in a grotesque sense of the word. He guessed the dead man had been killed some time ago, left in the cave by the Hunter to avoid being seen. The man was wearing some kind of uniform, though what kind he couldn't tell in the dark.

The footsteps drew nearer. Zack only had seconds to act. The killer would be on top of him in minutes. His face lined with disgust, Zack softly slid into the pool, making the softest splash. He ducked under the water and reluctantly pulled the floating corpse over him.

***

Rodney Crowe thought he heard something moving deeper in the cave. He advanced, holding the bow in front of him. His pistol remained available to him if he needed it, but the killer preferred his prey to suffer. The camper put out his eye, and for that there would be consequences. He'd hunted the man all the way to the cave before the trail had gone cold. Rodney grew impatient. He searched around the chamber with his infrared goggles, searching for some trace of life. Other than the occasional rat or group of bats, there was nothing. The killer rounded a corner and looked down, where he saw the dead body floating in the pool of water.

***

Zack forced himself to keep holding his breath, though he knew he would need to surface eventually. The killer was looking straight at him. He could feel his skin crawl. Time seemed to freeze. A thousand thoughts and emotions raced through his head at once. Most were about Lily. Zack thought he would welcome an end to his pain, but as he stared death in the face, he realized that he very much wanted to live.

All of the guilt he had allowed to fester inside him day after day threatened again to rise to the surface. The regret, the pain, it was all there. This time, as he held his breath under the water, he listened to Cole's words, and he let it all go.

Lily, he thought, *I forgive you.* In doing so, he forgave himself.

After what seemed like an eternity, the killer turned his head and looked at something else. Zack watched as the man knelt down, picked up the two-way radio, and retreated into the darkness.

Zack rose to the surface and gulped in a fresh lungful of air. He waited a few minutes until he thought it was safe before pulling himself out of the pool, leaving the bloated corpse behind. His knee scraped against the unforgiving rock. It struck Zack as odd that the killer bothered to retrieve the broken walkie-talkie. It wasn't of use to him, not broken. How had he even spotted the device in the first place?

He took a step forward. His left leg made a faint splashing noise as it left the water. Ahead, the sound of the killer's footsteps grew soft. Having failed to find Zack, the man would either keep looking elsewhere or return to deal with Beth and Will. The two had a sizable head start, but the killer had obviously spent time learning the park well. There was also likely a contingency plan in place in case they returned to the lodge.

The killer's shadow disappeared just around a corner. Then Zack spotted a large rock resting on the floor of the cave. There was a way to keep the killer off his friends' trail. Zack slid his hand along the surface of the ground and picked up the jagged stone. He crept toward the entrance of the cave and looked for a sign of the killer. The footsteps died away, leaving silence in their wake. The storm had finally passed, at least for the moment.

Zack took a few deep breaths and gathered his courage. There was no coming back from this. He closed his eyes and jumped into the moonlight, holding the stone high.

The killer was nowhere in sight. Zack started to search for a way back to the trail when he spotted something in the mud. It was a boot print. The killer had left it behind. Zack paused for a moment, before quickly following the tracks. They would lead him right to the killer and to his friends. The Hunter was about to become the hunted.

***

Rodney Crowe had almost shouted in anger when he spotted the radio inside the cave. His prey eluded him again. The killer wasn't used to being denied. Most of his victims were easy targets who put up little struggle. It didn't matter. He would find the camper who had blinded him, and he would make him suffer.

The killer checked the time. Day wouldn't arrive for another few hours. The game was still going on, and he intended to win. He knew where the remaining campers were headed. As Crowe stepped onto a secret trail known only to him, he imagined the various painful ways he would kill them to make them pay for what their friend had done to his eye.

The night wasn't over yet.

CHAPTER SEVENTEEN

4:38 AM

"**I** THINK WE SHOULD GO BACK for Zack."

It wasn't the first time Beth had suggested this. Will wasn't sure how much more of it he was going to put up with.

"I heard you the first time," he said irritably, continuing on what was proving to be the aptly named Endless Trail. Will marched on, with Beth trailing closely behind.

"What if he needs us?"

Will came to a stop and stared his companion down with the darkest expression he could muster. The woman remained undeterred.

"You heard the gunshots. How can you just leave him? He's your friend."

This was as far as Beth got. Will reached out and grabbed her by the arm, squeezing tightly. "I know. And if I could leave him behind, what do you think that means for you if you don't keep your mouth shut?" Beth's eyes flashed in anger under the moonlight. In another place and time, Will might have found this attractive. At the moment, he found Beth's behavior endlessly annoying. "Besides," he said more quietly. "We're being followed."

He'd known for some time that someone was on their trail. So far, there was enough of a lead for him to be reasonably sure of their safety. That could soon change.

"How can you be so heartless?"

He didn't answer the question. Leaving Steve behind hadn't bothered him because the man was already dying. Sacrificing Cole to save himself was necessary, and while it had initially troubled him, he was now numb to it. Surviving was everything. It meant more than friendship, more than morality. Cole would have sneered at the idea, but Cole was likely dead and Will was alive. Now Zack was probably dead as well. Will and Beth had heard the gunshots from Whispering Reach, though they were too far away to see what transpired. In either event, Zack had managed to come through for him one last time. His friend distracted the killer long enough for them to get a head start back to the lodge. The rain slowed them down a little, but now the clouds were moving away and the moon was out again.

Will estimated they still had a half-hour or so before they reached the lodge. He'd led Beth off the trail, despite her insistence against it. She'd worried they would get lost. Will glanced at her again as they resumed the trek. When she occasionally gazed his way, it was with nothing but contempt.

Why am I even keeping her around? he wondered. With Zack dead, Will's promise to protect her no longer mattered. Maybe it would be easier to cut her loose and leave her as another distraction for the killer. He smiled at the idea before quickly deciding against it. Beth was a second set of hands, which might come in handy if he needed her help. If the killer found them, well, he'd certainly have a far easier time sacrificing her than he had with Cole.

Will looked to the large moon for reassurance. He basked in the light, which he knew would guide him to safety and rest—much like the nightlight kept in his room as a child. The cell phone sat ready in his back pocket in case the darkness threatened to overwhelm him again. He took it out and flipped it open. There was still no reception. Will returned the phone to his pocket and held on tightly to the shotgun. The killer caught him off guard the last time, and Will had clearly missed his target. He swore to himself that wouldn't happen again.

A few minutes later he saw it through the trees, clear as day, basking in the light of the moon.

"The lodge," he whispered. He reached out with his free hand, as if to touch it. The building was almost two miles from the hilly terrain at the beginning of the Endless Trail. Beggar's Road loomed below, which led from the lodge toward Whispering Reach. It was the road they'd first taken to their campground hours earlier. That felt like a lifetime ago now.

***

"What now?" Beth asked. She tried to keep her tone neutral. The edge in her companion's voice was causing her to feel seriously uneasy. Given what else lurked in the forest, that was saying something.

"We'll take the long way around," Will said softly, almost to himself. "We'll reach the building from behind, using the forest as cover."

Beth wasn't sure of this plan. She'd seen the traps in the forest. She remembered what happened to Ron. In her gut, Beth suspected the killer had a plan in place in the event one of the campers reached the lodge.

"What about the dock?" she asked. "It's not far from the lodge."

Will looked at her as if she were crazy. "We're not risking being exposed just so we can get to some boats that may not even have fuel in them. The lodge will have working phones, and if not, I'll be close enough to the road to use my cell phone."

Will was hoping someone had left their keys at the lodge, but Beth found the possibility unlikely. Now that Zack was out of the picture, their plan to use the van was no longer feasible.

Beth hesitantly followed Will farther away from the trail. For a while, she had truly convinced herself that everything was going to work out. Zack had checked in with them every so often, shining his flashlight down from the peak. When he reached the top, Beth found herself holding her breath. As she crouched in the bushes waiting with Will, she had finally started to relax. Then the sound of gunshots echoed above the thunder. Beth felt her skin crawling just thinking about it.

She looked again at Will. He seemed surprisingly unaffected by his friend's death. The man she was with now under the cover of darkness stood in sharp contrast with the one who had flirted with her earlier that day in front of Ron. There was something in his eyes that made her uncomfortable. He was slowly becoming unhinged right in front of her.

"Come on," her companion said.

Will carefully made his way down the steep incline where erosion had eaten away the hillside, exposing mud and rocks. He extended his hand and helped her down, all the while looking past her beyond the forest. Having taken his eye off the ground, Will stumbled and slid down the hill. He landed softly in the mud at the foot of the hill. Beth stood above him, holding onto a small tree for support. She reached for the shotgun, which had slipped out of his grip.

Will's eyes grew wide. "Don't touch that," he said in a hiss.

Before she could respond, the sound of dry leaves crunching sounded nearby.

Someone was coming. Beth saw a dark figure emerging from the trees below, approaching Will. Dizzy from the fall, Will tried to regain his footing, but slipped and fell back against the muddy earth. The figure drew nearer. Pale light glinted off the handgun the man was holding. Will reached into his pocket and grabbed the cell phone. He pointed the light at the intruder as if warding off an evil spirit. The light did nothing to deter their silent stalker, who was almost on top of him.

A shotgun blast echoed across the trail.

"Stop right there!" shouted Beth, who had fired the shot. The figure looked up and saw her holding the shotgun on him. "Don't come any closer!"

In response, the man held his hands in the air, as if in surrender. Beth noted that he continued holding onto the gun.

"It's okay," the man said. "I'm not here to hurt you." He stepped into the moonlight.

It was Austin Fields. Beth's mouth dropped open in surprise.

"Thank God," she whispered. She lowered the shotgun.

The park ranger let out a sigh of relief and returned his handgun to its holster. As Beth made her way down the hill, Fields helped Will out of the mud.

"Thanks," Will said flatly, a vacant expression on his face.

"You're alive!" Beth exclaimed. Fields turned to face her while listening for sounds in the forest behind them. "We saw your vehicle turned over on the trail. We thought something had happened to you."

"It almost did," Fields muttered.

"Where were you?" Will demanded. He snatched the shotgun back from Beth, now clearly angry. "We tried radioing in, but you never answered. Why did you give us those things in the first place if you couldn't even be bothered to pick up?"

Fields glared at Will, and Beth could sense that the camper had picked the wrong person to tangle with. Will probably sensed it too, because he quickly backed down.

"Believe me, I was on my way," the ranger answered. "Hickory Johnson wasn't answering his phone, and I couldn't find him at the lodge."

"Did you call the police?" Beth asked hopefully.

Fields shook his head. "I decided to check the trails first. I heard your group radioing in, but couldn't make out what you were saying. When I tried contacting you, no one answered. Then I overturned my ATV in the mud. I finally found your trail earlier, and I've been following you since then."

"Everyone else is dead," Will said. "The Hunter came into our tent and killed one of my friends. Then he blew up my friend and a poacher we found next to the river. He killed my other friends, and her boyfriend," he said, animatedly gesturing at Beth. "We're the only ones left."

"Get a hold of yourself," Fields said sternly. "The only way we'll all get out of this is if we stick together."

"We're headed for the lodge," Beth interrupted. "We're going to try to find a phone or a car to get out of here."

Fields nodded. "That's a good idea. The keys to my car are still on my desk."

"Then what are we waiting for?" Will demanded. "Let's go."

"Okay. I'll cover you," the park ranger said, facing the rear. "Whoever's hunting us will have heard the blast from your shotgun."

Beth looked over her shoulder nervously before nodding in agreement. The trio began making their way through the sparse edge of the forest toward the lodge. There was only one way to go now, and that was forward. Beth occasionally glanced back and forth at her two companions. Will seemed somewhat stabilized by the park ranger's appearance, though he continued to hold the shotgun so tightly his knuckles were white. Fields kept a watchful gaze trained on the forest behind them. Beth thought he looked distracted, like something else was weighing on his mind.

She tried telling herself that with two guns, they were more than a match for the Hunter, but she couldn't shake the feeling something was very wrong. She regretted firing the shotgun into the air, which probably alerted the killer to their path.

"We're almost there," Fields said a short time later.

They huddled at the edge of the forest and stared at the specter of the dark lodge. Clouds were once again beginning to conceal the moon. Beth prayed more rain wasn't on the way.

Fields turned to Will. "See if the back door is unlocked. I'll stay here and keep watch." He took out his gun. "You stay here with me," he said to Beth. "If anything happens, run to the lodge."

"It should be her," Will protested. "She should go."

"You're the one with the gun," Fields said. The park ranger gritted his teeth, and Will relented. He emerged from the woods and slowly crept toward the lodge. A short distance later he reached the back door.

So far, so good, Beth thought. She watched as Will tried opening the door. It was locked.

He turned around, looking to Fields for guidance. Under the cover of night, it was hard to see them from the lodge.

Then Beth heard the gunshot. The bullet splintered the wooden façade of the building just next to the door. Beth saw Will's mouth drop in horror. He glanced into the forest surrounding him on three sides. The shot could have come from anywhere.

Beth watched as Will shot the door with the shotgun. He smashed through the frame and spilled into the darkness inside.

"Go after him," Fields said, turning around. "Run!"

"Don't leave us!" Beth begged. She grabbed his arm tightly.

Fields looked her over for a moment and pulled his arm free.

"I'll be back," he said before vanishing into the trees.

Her heart pounding, Beth took off for the lodge. The roar of another gunshot echoed loudly behind her. She was dimly aware of the bullet passing through her leg before she felt the pain. Beth stumbled and fell to the ground. She could see Will in the doorway, watching her from the darkness. His eyes gleamed in the pale light.

"Help me," she begged.

He watched her for another moment before turning and disappearing into shadow. Beth glanced over her shoulder. She couldn't see any sign of the killer out there, but she knew he was there all the same. Fighting through the pain, she clawed her way toward the door.

***

Rodney Crowe licked dry lips. He watched the woman crawling slowly closer to the safety of the lodge through his one good eye. She would never set foot in the lodge alive. He would see to that.

The killer took aim with the rifle and prepared to take the shot. He was done playing games. His finger slid over the trigger.

At that moment, Zack stepped out from behind him and bashed the killer's head with a sharp rock. Disoriented, Crowe dropped the gun. It fell down the hill out of his reach. He tasted blood.

"You," the killer whispered. He pulled the hunting knife free and pointed at the camper. "I'm going to make you wish you were never born."

Zack rushed the man before he had a chance to do anything else. He smashed the killer's face with the rock, knocking several of his teeth out. The killer collided with him, and the two rolled down the hill and fell apart. Crowe jumped to his feet, still gripping the knife. Zack regained his footing and looked for a way out. He saw something gleaming on the ground in the moonlight and moved sideways, keeping his eyes on the killer.

"Do it," he muttered. "If you think you can."

The killer spit out blood and fragments of broken teeth before rushing toward him. Zack pivoted, and the killer reached out with the knife.

The bear trap snapped shut around Crowe's leg. Zack could hear the sound of bone breaking. The killer was caught in one of his own traps. Zack didn't stick around long enough to see what the killer would do next. He took off running toward the lodge, to freedom.

Rodney Crowe watched the camper until the man disappeared from sight. His legs buckled. Crowe forced himself forward, his mangled leg dragging behind him along the ground.

I'll kill them, he thought amid the pain. *I'll kill them all.*

Crowe's face was covered in the blood of his ruined eye and

missing teeth. The blood sparkled in the moonlight. He hobbled along, knife in hand. It was all he could do to keep his balance. The bear trap clanged against the earth where he'd uprooted it. The metal teeth pinched his leg more with each step.

A form moved in the forest ahead of him. The killer gritted stained teeth and readied his knife. When he looked up, the figure was gone.

"You let them get the best of you."

The cold words cut him. Crowe spun around, wincing from the pain in his leg. The Hunter stood before him. Crowe lowered the knife. The man watched him with black eyes.

"Look what they've done to me," Crowe said. "And now they're at the lodge. We have to take them now. Together."

The Hunter moved closer to him. Crowe could smell the man's foul breath on his face. Under the moonlight, the Hunter's silver necklace seemed to glow with an eerie hue.

"You're too injured to finish the hunt," he whispered. His words sounded like a hiss. "Your blood is everywhere. The authorities will find you, and they'll make you talk."

Crowe's lower lip started to quiver. He kept the knife clenched tightly in his hands. "I won't say anything."

His friend smiled. "No. You won't."

Crowe tried thrusting the knife into the man's side, but the Hunter was ready for him. He caught Crowe's wrist and snapped it like a twig. The blade fell to the ground, and Crowe sank to his knees.

The Hunter stared down at his protégé with a slight feeling of disappointment and picked up the hunting knife.

"Did you really think you could play this game and never become a part of it?" he asked while spinning the knife in his fingers.

Before Crowe could answer, the Hunter cut his throat. He could hear the whispers murmuring in approval. In death, his friend would still have a purpose. When the police came, they would find Rodney Crowe's body. The serial killer responsible for dozens of deaths in state parks around the country would finally be laid to rest. The case would be closed, and after enough time had passed, the Hunter would resume his deadly game.

Only one thing remained. There were still campers left alive.

It was time to finish the game.

CHAPTER EIGHTEEN

5:00 AM

TEARS STUNG HER EYES. BETH'S fingernails scraped against the black pavement, producing a shrill sound that echoed in her ears. Ahead, the empty doorway beckoned elusively where Will had stood only seconds before.

"Help me," she cried again. She hoped a sudden surge of conscience would compel Will to return, but no form appeared in the darkness of the doorway. She was alone. Each second felt like an eternity. The distance to the lodge, ordinarily an easy one, seemed vastly magnified. Beth was exposed under the full light of the moon. Any second now the next bullet would echo, and that would be it.

Blood poured from her leg. Oddly enough, the pain felt muted. Instead, her entire body burned like it was on fire. Her strength threatened to give way, but Beth renewed her efforts to crawl to the lodge's entrance.

Someone was moving in the brush near the forest behind her. Beth's hair stood on end. Her shallow breathing sounded like the thunder of drums. A shadow materialized on the lodge wall against the backdrop of the moonlight. He had come for her.

Don't look back, she thought. Beth trained her sights on the door, which slowly but surely drew closer. *You can make it,* she thought, repeating the mantra over and over inside her head. *You can do it.* She quickened her pace.

It was too late. A hand grabbed her from behind. Fingers gripped her shoulder tightly, and Beth screamed.

"It's okay," Zack whispered. "I'm here."

"Zack?" Beth replied weakly. Zack looked like he'd been through a war since they'd parted. He was covered in mud and debris, and his clothes were torn.

***

"Relax," he said. He quickly glanced over his shoulder at the woods before returning his attention to her. Based on what happened minutes earlier, he doubted the killer would be catching up to them anytime soon. Nevertheless, he didn't want to take any chances.

Beth turned over, and he spotted her leg.

"What happened?" he asked.

"I've been shot," she whispered. Her voice was faint.

"Join the club," Zack muttered. "Come on," he added as he helped Beth to her feet. "We've got to get you inside." She leaned against his shoulder, and Zack put his arms around her. They walked toward the lodge, Beth hobbling on one leg.

If the frayed wooden lodge seemed creepy to the campers the previous morning, in the darkness it was like something out of a nightmare. Shadows twisted around each unfamiliar corner. Pictures and photographs mounted on the walls were disfigured by the blackness. What little moonlight filtered into the lodge served only to highlight the grotesqueries lurking within.

It was quiet. Zack watched Beth's blood drip onto the wooden floor. He eased her to the floor and propped her against a wall.

"What are you doing?" she asked, a faint hint of panic in her voice.

"Closing the door," he said. Zack tried his best to shut the splintered door to seal away the horrors outside. "What happened? Where's Will?"

He found a table in the adjoining snack room and pushed

it against the door. The sound of the wind banging against the doorframe died down.

"He left me," Beth said. "He saw me get shot, and he vanished in here."

"That bastard," Zack muttered.

Will had always had a cold side, but this was a part of his friend he'd never seen before. Turning his attention back to Beth, he smashed through the glass of a drink machine in the snack room and retrieved a bottle of water. He paused on the way back. Something caught his eye outside one of the windows, where a dark shape moved outside the screen.

It's just a tree, Zack realized. *Pull yourself together.*

"Here," he said, handing her the water. "Drink this. You're losing fluids."

Beth grabbed the bottle and almost drained it in seconds. "There's something else," she said. "We found Fields. When the shooting started, he ran into the forest after the killer. I haven't seen him since."

There was fear in her voice. Zack wanted to tell her about his confrontation with the killer, but didn't want to raise her hopes in case the man returned. He couldn't put the killer's green eyes out of his mind, and how different they were from the black eyes of the man who'd held a knife to his throat in the tent.

He studied her wound in the dim light. "It looks like the bullet passed through." Although her leg was covered in blood, it appeared the projectile had actually entered her lower thigh. "I need to find some bandages," he whispered. "And a phone."

Beth's eyes grew wide in the darkness. "Don't leave me here," she pleaded.

"I can't take you with me. Not yet." Zack handed her another bottle of water. "You need to rest." He hated the idea of leaving her alone in the hallway, but he couldn't think of any better options. He could move a lot faster unhindered. "I'll be back soon. I promise."

Zack made his way farther into the lodge, which seemed far more expansive in the dark. The cool air gave him the chills. He soon found himself standing in the main hall. Eyes of animals long dead followed him as he wandered down the hall, aware of their frozen gazes. The mounted animals somehow appeared even more menacing than before. A flight of stairs loomed at the end of the hallway. Zack had forgotten where they led. He didn't intend to venture any farther into the darkness than he had to.

Moonlight filtered through the windows over Fields' empty desk. Zack wondered if the park ranger was still alive. He reached the gift shop and peered into the room through the glass door. There was a shelf covered by medicines and bandages. He tried opening the door, which was locked. Taking a plaque from the wall, Zack shattered the glass door. He clenched his teeth at the loud sound and stepped inside the room. Even the stuffed toy bears took on a sinister appearance under the cover of night. Zack quickly grabbed a handful of bandages.

The floorboards squeaked back in the main hall. Zack froze. He crept back into the hall, walking softly so that the floor wouldn't creak under his weight.

"Is anyone there?" he called. "Beth? Will?" Other than the taxidermied animals, he was alone.

On the way back, he spotted a phone on Hickory Johnson's desk. Zack ran over to the desk and set the bandages down. His hand shaking, he reached out and lifted the phone.

"It won't work," a voice said flatly behind him. Zack jumped. A figure was staring at him in the dark. "I already tried it."

"Will?"

"He cut the power," Will said. Moonlight spilled into the room, illuminating Will's face. Zack didn't like what he saw. His friend's eyes were manic, his grip on the shotgun constantly tightening.

"Will, are you okay?"

Will stopped and looked around suddenly. "He's here," he whispered.

Zack shook his head. "I left him in the forest. He was wounded."

Will gritted his teeth, and his eyes darted around the room.

"Did you hear that?" he asked.

"What?"

"It's like a whisper," Will muttered. "Burrowing its way into my head. We need to get out of here."

Zack held up the bandages. "Beth's hurt. She needs our help. How could you just leave her there?"

"Don't look at me like that," Will said angrily. His voice rose, and he began making animated gestures with the shotgun. "Don't you dare judge me. You would have done the same thing. We're survivors, Zack. Now if you're not coming with me, get out of my way."

"You're not going anywhere. We have to stick together. You have the shotgun."

Anger flashed across Will's face. "I'm getting sick and tired of this. You think that just because your girlfriend cheated on you, that gives you the right to point the finger at everyone else?"

Thunder echoed outside the lodge, a faint reminder that the storm wasn't over yet. Will blinked and seemed to realize what he'd just said.

"I never told anyone that Lily cheated on me," Zack said. The two men circled each other. "Anyone."

Just like that, it all clicked. Will, who had frequently complained that he'd set his sights on Lily first. Will, the woman-chaser who could never handle not getting his way. Zack had told Will everything about Lily. His friend had gotten to know all of her flaws and vulnerabilities, and then he used her, just like he used everyone else. Anger rose within Zack like a blazing torch.

Will silently slipped off the shotgun's safety and took a few steps back. "Zack, it was just one time."

"I'm going to kill you," Zack roared.

He lunged forward. Will raised the shotgun and pulled the trigger. Nothing happened. The gun had jammed. Will felt Zack's weight slam into his body, pushing him against the desk. Papers spilled to the floor. Zack tightened his hands around Will's neck. Will gasped for air and swung the shotgun at Zack's head. Zack stumbled back, and Will took aim again with the shotgun. Before he could pull the trigger, Zack was on him again. He tackled Will, and they stumbled back over the edge of the staircase. With one hand on Zack and one on the shotgun, Will couldn't steady himself in time. The two men rolled down the stairs toward the unknown.

***

She stared at what was left of the door. Beth couldn't bring herself to tear her eyes away from the splintered frame. Outside, the wind had picked up again, blunting itself against the lodge's exterior. The table held the door in place, but Beth kept watching the door, waiting for something to happen.

Her wet hair and clothes had long since started to dry. She knew she should be tired. Instead, Beth was fully alert. Her heart was pumping faster than she thought possible. Zack was taking too long. She was scared. She couldn't bring herself to look down at her thigh, not that she would be able to see the damage in the darkness anyway. That's when she heard the raised voices. Her hair stood on end.

She turned her head back to the hallway and listened quietly. She recognized one of the voices. It was Zack. He was talking to someone.

The door rattled loudly behind her. Beth screamed. Someone was trying to force his way inside the lodge. The splintered door shook, barely held in place by the desk. The door thudded again and again. Finally it fell still. Beth realized she'd been holding in her breath. She exhaled and moved closer to the door. Was the intruder gone?

"Zack?" she called.

The door rattled loudly again, inches from her face. Beth screamed. A hand attempted to slip inside the door. Beth grabbed the edge of the table and pulled herself up. The pain was overwhelming. She limped backwards, watching the door shake. As she moved into the next hall, the door started to give way.

"Zack!" she shouted. There was no response. She leaned against the wall for support and hobbled forward, looking for a place to hide. Beth spotted a closet. She tugged on the handle, which was locked. She pulled harder. The door sprung open, dumping a form out at her feet. As the moonlight sprinkled inside the lodge, she could see she outline of an old man stuffed into the closet, his face frozen in fear. He was dead. Beth screamed.

She hurried into a room covered with mounted animals. Beth spotted packages of bandages on the ground. She scooped them up quickly and kept moving. The moon vanished into the clouds again, and the room was covered in darkness. Footsteps echoed down the hall. Beth slipped into a dark room near the end of the hall, stepping over broken glass. She crouched against one of the shelves at the back of the room, praying she couldn't be seen amid the blackness. She opened the package and started wrapping the bandages around her thigh. Her heart pounded heavily in her chest.

The floor creaked in the hallway. Someone was in the lodge with her. Beth heard the footsteps grow closer. She tried to slow her breathing down, hoping the intruder couldn't hear her. Glass crunched under the man's boots. Beth couldn't get a good look at him over the shelves in the pitch-black room. He wandered down the shelves one row over from her. If he walked to the next row, it was over. She was right around the corner.

A loud thump sounded below. The man turned and glanced off in the opposite direction. He walked away, and the floorboards creaked under his weight. Beth let out a sigh of relief. She pulled herself up and stared over the shelves. There was no sign of the intruder. Beth fumbled through the products on the shelves and found a lighter. The glow of the flame wasn't nearly as strong as the flashlight she'd lost, but it was better than walking around blindly.

Below her, the sound rumbled again. Something was happening below. Beth didn't know what to do. Should she stay where she was and wait for daylight? Or should she try to find Zack? She bit her lip. Zack hadn't abandoned her when she needed him. Beth took a few steps forward and looked for the stairs.

***

"Is that all you've got?" Will asked. He wiped blood from his chin. Zack was on the ground, reeling. They'd fallen into a game room. Will got up first and kicked Zack in the side. Zack's chest erupted with pain. Will grabbed him and threw him against the pool table.

"You took everything from me," Zack muttered. He reached backwards until his hand closed around a pool ball. When Will struck at him, he smashed the ball against Will's jaw. Zack struck his friend in the gut, and Will slammed into the ping-pong table.

Will knocked Zack's legs out from under him. He punched Zack's chest again and again, while Zack tried his best to protect his face. The shotgun rested on the staircase, just out of reach. Zack smashed his head against Will's forehead. Will stumbled back, and Zack snatched the shotgun and aimed it at Will's chest.

"You could have had anyone you wanted," he whispered. He eased his finger against the trigger. "Why couldn't you have just left her alone?"

Will didn't reply. He only watched Zack with a look of pure loathing. Zack's entire body trembled with rage. He hesitated. Somehow Zack knew that taking Will's life wouldn't end the pain, the suffering, or the regret. Only he could choose to make a new start for himself—or condemn himself forever. He stared at Will, the shotgun shaking in his hands. Finally, he lowered the gun, disgusted at his own rage and hatred.

"You're not worth it," he muttered.

Sensing his opportunity, Will lunged forward. Zack hit him in the face with the barrel of the shotgun. He stood over Will and watched him with narrowed eyes.

"We're done. You can find your way out of this on your own."

Will started whimpering. "Don't leave me here alone. Not alone in the dark." He sounded like a frightened child.

"Zack," a soft voice said from the stairs. It was Beth. "We need to go," she said. "He's here. In the lodge." She looked from Zack to Will, as if trying to piece together what had just happened.

Zack nodded. "Come on." He took her hand and didn't give Will another look. The two headed up the stairs, leaving the man behind them sitting alone in the dark.

***

The pair managed to surprise the Hunter, something that rarely happened. Instead of heading for the front door, they made their way out the back entrance. They weren't heading for the road at all. Where were they going?

"The lake," he muttered. The pair was heading down another trail, another route that would take them back to Dire Lake. It was one of the few places he hadn't set any traps. He would have to pursue them on foot. The Hunter frowned when he noticed that Zack was holding Will's shotgun. The killer glanced at the sky. It wouldn't be long before dawn, and he was running out of time.

The Hunter returned his gaze to the lodge. He would follow the two remaining campers to the dock and finish his work there. Before that, however, he had another matter to attend to.

CHAPTER NINETEEN

5:37 AM

As Cole predicted hours ago, the cell phone's battery was dying. It didn't matter. Soon Will would be close enough to the road to either find a signal or someone willing to give him a ride. Who needed Zack? Let them scurry off to wherever. He didn't care. Will limped up the steps, using the phone's light to guide him as he held on to the guardrail. His body ached in pain.

For a moment, he really thought Zack was going to kill him. Will had certainly been willing to pull the trigger himself. He no longer felt any remorse. He just wanted to survive. The battery sign was flashing across the screen in an attempt to warn him the cell phone's energy was depleted. If it could just keep going a little longer, he would be safe.

Lily had never held any special meaning for him. She was just one among a countless number of women who meant nothing to him. He'd found her alone and needy, and he did what came naturally to him. Lily's own particular brand of self-destruction took it from there. It wasn't his fault, and it wasn't his problem.

If only he'd reached the shotgun first.

"Screw Zack," he muttered, hobbling to Fields' desk. He'd sprained his ankle during the fight.

Will grinned when he spotted the keychain. The keys were on

the desk, just like the park ranger promised they would be. Will snatched them off the desk. Let Zack and his little girlfriend slink off somewhere else. The Hunter would find them and kill them. As for himself, Will intended to get as far away from Drifter's Folly as he could as soon as possible. He rehearsed his story, thinking of what he would tell the police. When it was all over, maybe he'd even be viewed as a hero.

A whisper echoed behind him, and Will wheeled around.

"Who's there?" he demanded, shining the cell phone's light toward the back of the room. There was nothing there. He heard it again. "Shut up!" Will shouted, his voice full of rage. "Stop it!"

The room fell silent. He was alone. Will's heart thudded in his chest. He was starting to lose it, just like Zack.

I have to get out of here, he thought.

Will returned to the entrance hall and stood at the front door, the cell phone in one hand and the keys in the other. He hesitated for a moment. Despite what Zack said about leaving the killer behind in the forest, Will hadn't survived this long without being cautious. As he waited in the dark, anxiety got the better of him, and Will took a deep breath and swung the door open.

The mostly empty parking lot sat under the shadow of the mountains. Moonlight reflected off vehicles resting idly on black pavement. At the end of the parking lot, a mesh fence closed off the area. Will spotted his van as he scanned the area for Fields' vehicle. He saw the vehicle in a lot closest to the fence. Casting one last glance at the distant forest overlooking the lodge, Will exhaled and started limping toward the parking lot as fast as he could.

As he crossed the threshold of the lodge, a solitary bar appeared on the cell phone. Will's heart soared. He punched in 911 and kept moving, never taking his eyes off the van's shimmering metal exterior. He was free.

"911, what is your emergency?"

"I'm in the park," he stammered. "Someone's trying to kill me!"

"Where are you, sir?"

"Drifter's Folly Memorial Park," he repeated, limping toward the vehicle.

"Are you injured? Is anyone else with you?"

Before he could reply, Will's foot tripped over a wire strung across the ground. In his haste to reach the van, he hadn't noticed the wire. The Hunter had left one last trap, and he'd walked right into it.

Will took off, running for the fence. His ankle was slowing him down. He heard the first explosion behind him and felt its searing heat as the van erupted in flame. Another car exploded, and another. Each car across the entire parking lot was rigged to blow, like a set of dominos.

The operator's voice had fallen silent. Will reached the mesh fence and tried to scale it. He couldn't make it to the top. The final explosion knocked him against the pavement. Something heavy landed on him, pinning him to the ground. Columns of thick, black smoke rose into the air. The remains of the cars were covered in flame. Will's eardrums had burst. Blood poured out of his mouth, and several of his bones were broken.

He tried moving the deformed metal husk pinning him to the ground, but it was no use. Will's head was spinning. Then he saw the man walking toward him across the parking lot, and he knew. It was the same look he'd seen reflected in his own eyes in the game room's mirrors.

"You," he tried to say. Instead, he coughed more blood out of his mouth.

The Hunter had come to claim him. Will shook in fear, gripping the cell phone. He tried shining its light to scare away the monster, but no light came. The cell phone was dead.

He started shaking. "Please don't," he begged. "Please don't kill me."

The Hunter smiled and pulled out the same knife he'd used to kill Rodney Crowe. The camper screamed.

When he was finished, the killer crossed the parking lot until he reached the one truck left untouched by the explosion. It was the only vehicle he'd left unrigged. The Hunter swung the door open and stepped inside. He slid the key into the ignition and the engine fired to life. He felt for the gun at his side. He was finished with arrows and traps. It was time to end this.

Two left.

***

They were almost a mile from the lodge when the explosion rattled the night sky.

"What was that?" Beth asked. Zack could see pillars of smoke rising above the trees.

Will, he thought briefly.

"Come on," he said. "We have to keep moving." Beth was moving on her own now, without his help, but her injury was still slowing her down. Zack thought back to the man he left in the forest stuck in the bear trap. How had he gotten out?

"How does he keep finding us?"

There was desperation in her voice. The inner strength she'd displayed after Ron's death was starting to succumb to injury and fatigue.

"Don't worry," Zack whispered in an attempt to comfort her. "It's almost morning. We'll be safe once the sun rises. It won't be long until someone comes looking for us."

Though he didn't mention it to Beth, he *was* concerned with the killer's ability to track them. It was almost inhuman. Everywhere they had fled, the Hunter was always right behind. It didn't make any sense. What if Beth had been right hours earlier, when she'd suggested there was more than one person hunting them?

The pair wandered farther down the gravel-covered path that led downhill from the lodge. The moon peeked out from behind a wall of clouds, providing at least a small degree of illumination. Occasionally Zack caught himself looking back at the smoke.

"You were right not to make for the road," he said to Beth.

When she'd told him the killer was inside the lodge with them, every hair on the end of his back stood on end. Beth predicted that the Hunter would be waiting for them to run out of the front door toward freedom. Instead, she'd convinced him to exit the back and take another path.

"You're sure this way leads to the dock?" When they first drove into Drifter's Folly, Zack and the others had made for the campground right away. They hadn't bothered taking any of the other trails.

Beth nodded. "There's an old radio tower near the heart of the lake. We can radio for help. Ron and I almost rented a boat when we arrived. We drove down this road a few days ago." She sighed. "It feels like ages ago now."

Zack didn't like the weary look in her eyes. "Everything is going to be okay," he said reassuringly. "We just have to keep going a little longer."

The winding gravel road grew steeper in its descent. Zack felt a light mist around him, which was at least better than the rain.

"Would you have killed him?" Beth asked. "Your friend?"

Zack didn't reply for a few minutes. The sound of his shoes overturning gravel rocks was the only thing breaking the silence.

"No," he said. "Although in the end, he didn't turn out to be much of a friend." Zack wondered briefly if that was the killer's true goal: to reduce them all to animals willing to do anything to survive.

"You did the right thing."

Zack looked at Beth for a moment. He didn't have to say anything. He just nodded and kept on walking.

"Is that the dock down there?" Zack pointed at a shadowy

structure looming about a mile downhill. His legs burned with lactic acid buildup.

"I think so," Beth said. "It's hard to see in this fog."

Zack stopped dead in his tracks.

"Zack? What's wrong?"

A sound echoed in the distance, growing louder with each second. Zack paused and listened closer.

It was the sound of a diesel engine. He cast a glance over his shoulder. A truck was speeding toward them, kicking up a cloud of dust in its wake.

"Beth, run!"

The two raced down the hill. They weren't fast enough to match the speed of the truck, which gained on them with each second.

It's too far, Zack thought. *There's no way we'll reach the dock in time.*

"Go!" he shouted to Beth, pushing her in the direction of the trees just off the road. Standing his ground, he raised the shotgun into the air and pulled the trigger. The shell landed in the gravel next to the truck and missed by inches. The driver of the truck fired a gun in his direction several times in quick succession.

Zack turned and ran toward the trees. He could see Beth outpacing him near the edge of the forest. The driver floored the gas and wheeled his car off road. Caught in the headlights, Beth slipped over a rock and fell. The truck sped toward her with reckless abandon. The driver was going to run her down.

Zack pulled the trigger on the shotgun again. This time the shell shattered the truck's windshield. The driver kept going. The next shot missed. He was almost on top of Beth. Zack pulled the trigger one last time. The shell collided with the front left tire, and the driver lost control of the truck. It slid down the gravel road and into the fog. Zack heard a loud crashing sound seconds later.

"Beth!" Zack shouted. "Are you hurt?"

She shook her head, and he helped her to her feet.

Zack took her by the hand, holding the shotgun in the other. He didn't know how many shells remained in the weapon. There couldn't be many. They made their way down the hill amid the thick fog. He kept the gun outstretched, just in case. As they returned to the road, the sound of the whining engine grew louder.

The overturned truck had slammed into a tree. One of the headlights was broken; the other shone weakly into the lake, the beam vanishing into the black waters below.

"Be careful," Zack whispered as they neared the truck. Visible through the cracked window, the driver's seat was empty. The truck had been abandoned.

There was a small computer-like device in the front seat. Zack brushed it with the barrel of the shotgun.

"Hand me the lighter," he muttered.

Satellite Tracking Device, read the silver lettering.

Is that how he's been tracking us? A GPS device would make sense, but that didn't explain how the killer could track them all unless each camper was marked somehow or had a corresponding device.

The wind howled above the trees, and Zack looked up quickly. He handed the lighter back to Beth.

He's out there somewhere, Zack realized. It was just the three of them now, and the Hunter knew it.

"Stay behind me," he said to Beth. "We need to move quickly." He led her back into the woods.

"What are you doing?" she whispered. "We have to get to the lake."

"I know," Zack replied. "We can't take the road. We're too exposed. He could pick us off from the trees."

Moving toward the dock this way would be slower than on the road, but it was also safer. He held out his hand to Beth and helped her cross a log. Damp leaves attached themselves to his shoes. They were getting closer.

"Zack," Beth whispered. Her voice was filled with fear. "There's a man standing below us."

Zack froze. He followed Beth's gaze. A dark figure stood in the shadows of a tree below them. The man looked from side to side, as if waiting for them. Zack pulled Beth to the ground.

"Stay here," he whispered, advancing with the shotgun along the brush. He moved carefully and hoped the figure couldn't hear him.

The shadowy form turned around and looked back at the hill above. Zack could have sworn the figure looked right at him, but the man gave no sign at having seen him. Slowly, Zack raised the shotgun. There was no guarantee he would hit his target from that distance, but he couldn't risk getting any closer. As he eased his finger around the trigger, the moon glimmered off the weapon's barrel, and the figure saw him.

Under the moonlight, Zack recognized the man's uniform.

"Don't shoot!" the man shouted. "It's me!"

Zack recognized the voice.

"It's Fields," Beth whispered to him. The pair took off down the hill. The park ranger's clothes were torn and covered with dirt. "You made it," Beth said to Fields.

The ranger nodded. "I exchanged fire with someone in the woods, but he stopped shooting and I lost his trail. I'm glad you two are safe," he added. The park ranger looked at Zack and raised an eyebrow. "What happened to your friend?"

"He didn't make it," Zack replied flatly.

The wind picked up, which sent more leaves spilling down from the trees. In the darkness, they were all the same color.

The park ranger tensed. "We're not alone," Fields whispered. "There's someone in the forest with us."

"I know," Zack said. "We're on our way to the dock. If we can reach the radio tower, we should be able to call for help."

"It's too bad you don't have that radio I gave you," Fields said. "We're close enough you could probably reach someone that way."

"The lake is our only option left," Beth whispered. Her gaze was trained on the water below, less than a quarter-mile away.

"Then let's go," Fields said.

Zack was about to nod when he spotted the object exposed under the park ranger's collar. A layer of dark metal glowed softly in the moonlight. It was a necklace.

Zack remembered where he'd seen the necklace before, and every hair on his body stood on end. He could feel his heart echo within his chest. The truth hit him like a brick. It was Fields. It had been him all along. The park ranger was the one who told them about the Hunter in the first place.

The radios, he realized. *That's how he was following us.* Fields had handed them out to everyone during the day before. Each of the two-way radios had held a GPS unit inside, allowing the killer to track his prey wherever they fled to. It was why the other killer couldn't find Zack in the cave after Zack dropped his radio and left it behind when he hid. There were two killers from the start.

Fields followed Zack's gaze to the necklace. His eyes flickered up and met Zack's. A brief look of recognition flashed between the two men. Before Zack could move, the park ranger knocked him to the ground and grabbed Beth. Zack trained the shotgun on him, but Fields was holding a handgun firmly against Beth's head.

CHAPTER TWENTY

"**I**T WAS YOU," ZACK WHISPERED, somehow finding his feet. "It was you the whole time."

Fields' face had morphed into a monstrous visage. Even in the darkness, Zack could see evil in the man's eyes. Moonlight glinted off the killer's teeth as his lips curled up in a thin smile. Beth was trembling.

"Clever of you," Fields whispered. He took a step toward Zack, who held his ground.

"Don't come any closer!" he shouted.

"Or what? You'll shoot me?" Fields laughed. "I don't think so."

Zack kept his hands steady. "Who are you?"

The killer's black eyes gleamed in the darkness. "Not Austin Fields, at any rate. I killed him days ago and hid his body in a cave."

Zack suddenly realized the significance of the corpse he'd found in the cave, and the uniform it was wearing. 'Fields' had murdered the real park ranger and assumed his identity to explore the park without raising suspicion. Then he'd given all the campers two-way radios with GPS units installed so he could track them.

"Why are you doing this?"

Beth was crying now. The Hunter gripped her hair tightly with his free hand and jerked her head back to get her to stop struggling.

"You couldn't possibly understand."

"You weren't the man who followed me into the cave."

"That was Rodney Crowe," the killer muttered. "Don't worry, I finished your dirty work for you. He's dead now, something he has in common with all your friends. It was a game between us, to see who could kill the most people. A game you ruined." Contempt etched its way across the man's face.

"You're insane," Zack said.

"Perhaps," the killer answered. He took another step toward Zack. "What are you going to do about it?" He laughed. "You're weak. Just like your friends. If you really wanted to stop me, you'd put a bullet in me right now and walk away. But you won't do that, will you?" He jerked Beth's hair again. She screamed, and the Hunter grinned.

Zack saw the imposter Fields inching forward second by second, and he knew the killer was about to try something. His hands were shaking. If he pulled the trigger, he might hit Fields—but he might also hit Beth. He wouldn't get a second shot. The wind howled, hissing like hundreds of whispers. His pulse raced.

Suddenly, Beth tore free of Fields' grip long enough to sink her teeth into his forearm. The killer relinquished his grasp, and Beth threw herself forward.

Zack only had a split second to react. In that moment, he felt an invisible hand over his, steadying the shotgun. He squeezed the trigger. Fields reacted too slowly. The impact of the shell tearing into his chest drove him back against a tree. As Beth rushed to Zack's side, Zack pulled the trigger again. The gun didn't fire.

"It's empty," he muttered. He took Beth by the hand. "We have to go. Now." The two ran back toward the gravel road, out of the forest and into the fog.

***

The imposter Fields' body hung motionless against the tree for several moments longer. Suddenly, one of the killer's fingers twitched. Fields' eyes snapped open. He fell to his knees and let out a growl, ripping his button-up shirt and exposing the bulletproof vest underneath. The killer snarled. The shotgun's powerful kick had probably bruised—if not broken—at least one of his ribs.

He could still hear the couple running for the water. Fields rose from the ground and retrieved his gun. He would kill them for this. The necklace spilled out of his shirt, glowing faintly in the night. The Hunter didn't bother tucking it in. He would let them see. The skull would be the last thing they saw before he put the bullets in them.

The whispers echoed louder than ever. They were everywhere, behind every tree and in the wind itself. He put his hands to his head, fighting to get the voices to be quiet. This time it was harder to get them to obey. The blood he'd spilled had only given them an appetite for more. They were hungry, and so was he.

***

It remained too dark to tell if night was nearing its end, but Zack could feel it in his soul. A reckoning was coming. One way or the other, this was about to end.

The dock loomed just a few yards away. He could hardly see the dock in the thick fog, rising from the lake like a corpse from its slumber. Zack caught a brief glimpse of Beth out of the corner of his eye. She looked even more tired than he felt. They were both running on fumes.

"Just a little farther," he said softly. It seemed like he'd been saying that all night.

The mist clung to them, transiently caressing the two campers with ethereal tendrils. Zack's foot stepped off the gravel and landed on a hard surface. Beth took out the lighter and handed it to him. The 'dock' was a long splintered pier jutting out into the lake's black waters. A narrow roof mounted on rusted metal posts cloaked the first half of the pier in shadow. He took a few steps forward and almost tripped over a pile of faded rooftop tiles.

In the full light of the moon, Zack could see the dock for what it actually was: a graveyard. Planks of wood were missing or rotten. Several areas were closed off with ropes, presumably where boats could no longer dock. Most of the spaces for boats were empty. The boats that remained looked like they'd been left abandoned for years.

After spotting a boat that looked seaworthy, he ran over to it and tried to get it working.

"No keys," he muttered.

As he searched for keys, Beth began checking other boats. Zack's heart tightened in his chest. There weren't that many boats docked at the pier, period. He didn't want to dwell on what would happen if they ran out of likely candidates. Fields knew they were heading to the dock. With Fields in one direction and their backs against the lake, they were trapped. Hopefully, his gunshot had bought them enough time to find an alternate solution.

"Find anything yet?" he called. He tried to keep the panic from his voice. Beth didn't reply for a moment.

"Zack, I think we're in trouble."

He followed her gaze to an empty patch of fog on the hill leading to the dock, where a shadow moved through the mist along the gravel road. Zack's eyes grew wide. He ran farther down the pier, scanning the husks at either side for a usable vessel. Fields had almost reached the dock.

Zack was nearing the end of the pier when he spotted a small boat covered by a green tarp. He jumped next to the boat and pulled the tarp back. It was a small fishing boat with a crank-motor. The boat was covered in nets, coolers, and containers of gasoline.

"Beth!" he shouted. She rushed over to his side. "We have to try to start this thing." He jumped into the boat and yanked on the cord. Nothing happened.

Fields had reached the dock. Zack saw a gun in his hand.

He pulled the cord again with as much force as he could muster. This time, the engine made a sound.

"It's working!" Beth said. "Don't stop!" She was trying desperately to untie the boat from the dock.

Fields was advancing toward them, handgun raised. He pulled the trigger. The first bullet missed.

The engine roared to life, but Beth still hadn't freed the boat from the dock. Her hands slipped, and the killer drew nearer, seconds away from being within range. At the last moment, the knot came untied.

"Jump!" Zack hollered to Beth. When she started to jump into the boat, her injured leg fell through a rotten plank.

"Beth!" Zack shouted. He bounded off the boat and pulled her free. Fields was close enough that Zack could see his eyes shining in the moonlight. Without looking back, he helped Beth into the boat and jumped in after her.

The boat slowly sailed into the water. The vessel gained speed with each second, but it felt too slow to Zack. The imposter Fields was sprinting now, firing repeatedly. The gunshots echoed through the night sky as bullets sailed into the water, vanishing into the eerie depths of the lake.

Before they slipped under the cover of fog, Zack saw Fields watching them from the dock, a strange calm on his face. The Hunter let his empty handgun fall to the ground while he continued staring at them until they were out of sight.

They sailed in silence for several minutes. Zack tried to follow the pathway he thought would take them to the heart of the lake, but he had no idea if they were traveling in the right direction.

"What if he finds another boat?" Beth said after several minutes. She sat close to him; there wasn't much space on the small vessel that wasn't covered in nets and rope or junk.

"We have to focus on getting to the radio tower," Zack answered.

It wasn't long before a shimmering green light appeared through the fog. The light shone intermittently, blinking on and off every few seconds. As Zack guided the boat toward the light, a large tower emerged across the face of the dark, perched atop a small island randomly placed in the lake.

"That's it," Beth said. "That's the tower."

The structure took her breath away. They were almost there. The fog thinned the closer they got to the island. Zack spotted a dock near the shore and steered the boat in its direction. He tied the rope to the dock and helped Beth onto the shore. Together, they took the path leading to the tower. Situated on a rocky ledge, the tower looked down at Dire Lake like a silent guardian. The metal was twisted and covered with rust, yet another remnant of a forgotten time in the history of Drifter's Folly. The tower was covered in large windows shielding the dark contents within.

"We made it," Beth whispered. She leaned against him for support. There was a look of wonder in her eyes, like she'd been unexpectedly surprised in a good way. For a moment—just a moment—she looked like Lily.

"I told you we would. I promised to keep you safe." Beth looked at him quizzically. "Her name was Lily," he finally confessed. "I should've been there for her, and I wasn't. I thought if I saved you, maybe I could make up for it." Zack trailed off. They had reached the tower.

The door was unlocked and swung open almost as soon as he touched the knob. Zack led Beth up a winding staircase. The radio tower reminded Zack of a lighthouse he visited once as a child. At night, the tower seemed far less innocuous than the lighthouse he'd toured in the daytime. The metal steps creaked under his weight. By the time they reached the top, he was again out of breath.

"The equipment actually looks functional," Beth said. She almost smiled.

Zack nodded. The radios appeared new, as did all the other

systems on the wall. "Get on the computer. See if you can send a message. I'll try to use the radios."

To his surprise, he immediately received a response.

"Hello?" repeated a voice on the other end of the strong signal.

"This is Zack Allen," he said. "I'm in the radio tower of Drifter's Folly Memorial Park with another camper. Our friends are dead. We need help."

There was silence on the other end for a moment, and Zack feared he'd lost the signal.

"Police units have already been dispatched to the park," the voice said. "They should be arriving shortly."

Beth stood from the computer and took his hand. Her eyes welled up with tears.

Zack was stunned. The police were already on their way? How was that possible?

"How did you know to find us?" Zack asked.

Someone else must have already phoned in. Relief flooded through him, and he finally allowed himself to start feeling hope. He'd kept his word. They would live. He looked at Beth, and for the first time in a long time he smiled. He no longer wanted to just survive. Zack realized that he wanted to—he could—live again, truly live *for* something.

That was when he realized that there was still no response on the other end of the radio. Suddenly, all the lights in the tower went dead. Beth's grip on Zack's hand tightened.

"Zack, look." She pointed out the window. Down the path leading from the tower, below the window, they could see the dock. A jet ski was floating near the edge of the fog a short distance away from the boat. It was empty. Its rider was nowhere in sight.

"He's here," Zack whispered. His hair stood on end. He could feel Beth start to tremble against him. This couldn't happen now. They were so close. Help was on the way. Zack gritted his teeth. "We have to go," he said.

"No," Beth protested. "We need to find a place to hide."

"This island is small enough that he'll find us eventually. We have to get back to the boat. If we can reach the lodge, we should be able to wait for the police. They're already on their way."

Beth stared into his eyes as if searching for an answer to an unspoken question. "I'm scared."

"It's okay," he whispered reassuringly, squeezing her shoulder. "We're going to make it through this. I promise. You just have to be strong a little longer."

He took her by the hand and led her to the doorway. Zack peered down the staircase and searched for a sign of an intruder in the darkness. There was no trace of Fields. Zack and Beth slowly descended the winding staircase, careful to keep an eye out for the killer. Zack's heart was pounding. He half-expected the Hunter to spring from the shadows at any second. He winced when the rusty stairs again creaked under their feet.

The door remained open at the base of the staircase, allowing the faint moonlight to spill inside the dark tower.

"Let me go first," he said when they reached the bottom. "If Fields is waiting out there, he'll attack me first. If he does, you run for the boat as fast as you can."

"I'm not leaving you."

"Yes, you are," Zack replied forcefully. "If it comes to that." He hoped it wouldn't. There wasn't even a guarantee the boat would start again. Mustering his courage, Zack stepped out into the light.

He was alone. Zack returned to the radio tower. "On three, we're going to make a run for it."

Beth nodded. The look of determination had returned to her eyes.

Zack counted down, and the pair raced across the trail back to the boat. The fog had risen around the shore in their absence and virtually concealed the boat. Zack ran his hand along the rope until he found the small fishing vessel. He helped Beth into the boat and joined her.

"Here goes," he whispered. Starting the boat would inevitably warn Fields of their departure. It would be a race to get back to the lodge, though it was one he believed they would win. He pulled the cord and the engine roared to life.

They sailed through the fog, gaining momentum. Beth huddled close to him, and the two waited for a glimpse of shore.

***

Over the roar of the engine, Zack couldn't hear the sound of something scratching against the floor of the boat. A pile of nets and ropes moved behind him as a shadowy figure rose from his hiding place. The Hunter pulled his knife and watched the oblivious campers silently. They had taken the bait. He'd known they would. Now there was nowhere left for them to run. They were trapped on the boat, defenseless.

***

Zack felt something moving behind them. He glanced back just in time to see the Hunter swing his blade through the air.

"Beth!" he shouted, pushing her to the ground. The Hunter pinned Zack against the floor of the boat. He held the knife out, inching it closer to Zack's eye. Zack tried pushing him away, but the killer's strength was too much. The knife slid against his cheek, tearing into his flesh. Zack screamed.

Beth slammed the boat's lifebuoy against the killer's head. Snarling, the Hunter punched her in the stomach. The blow sent her sprawling against the deck, where her legs became entangled in the net. The killer raised his knife to finish her, and Zack plowed into him before he could stab her. The impact sent them both sprawling to the back of the boat, knocking over the containers of gasoline. The liquid spilled out over the deck.

As the Hunter started to stand, Zack went for the knife. The Hunter seized his arm, and the blade fell over the side of the boat, vanishing under the water as the boat picked up speed. Ahead, he could see the shore. At the rate they were moving, they would crash against the land if no one took the wheel.

He didn't have time to digest the sudden revelation. Fields grabbed him and pushed him against the back of the boat. Zack tried to fight back, but his fading strength was nothing compared to Fields'. The killer pushed his head down, closer to the motor. Zack's hand reached out in desperation and grabbed one of the gasoline containers. He slammed it against the killer's face, covering the man in the fluid.

"Beth," he shouted, "get off the boat!" The killer knocked him against the deck.

"I'm going to break her neck," the Hunter whispered, his hand on Zack's head. "I'm going to make you watch, and then I'm going to kill you." He slammed Zack's body against the deck again. Zack felt himself go limp. His head was spinning.

Beth had just freed herself from the net. They had almost reached the shore. The killer looked at her and smiled, his black eyes shining in the moonlight. Beth was paralyzed with fear. The Hunter stepped toward her, and his boot landed in a puddle of fuel.

"Over here," Zack said above the roar of the motor, loudly enough for the killer to hear.

Zack held the lighter in his hands. The flame flickered in the darkness. Before the Hunter could react, he threw the lighter against the deck at the killer's feet.

Zack saw Beth dive overboard just as the flames engulfed Fields. Zack jumped off the boat, which exploded, crashing against the shore. The impact rattled him, and Zack felt himself falling through the air. Suddenly, he felt the cold sensation of water covering him. Debris and fire rained down around him. He was vaguely aware that he was drowning, but that didn't matter now. Beth was going to live. He didn't have to fight anymore. He could finally rest. He closed his eyes.

A hand reached down into the darkness and pulled him up into the moonlight. He gasped for air, blindly spitting out water. He felt himself being paddled to shore. Soon he felt dry land under him.

"It's going to be okay," Beth whispered. "I've got you." Zack rested his head in her lap. He could hear sirens in the distance. Keeping Beth alive had given him a reason to live. In the end, *Beth* had saved *him*.

Zack would never know if it was his exhaustion, the mist, or something else, but for a moment he saw her in the fog, staring back at him from Dire Lake, and he thought he knew who had steadied his hands earlier.

"Goodbye, Lily," he mumbled, staring at the specter of the burning lake. Then he closed his eyes and slept.

EPILOGUE

THE DAY PASSED LIKE A dream—or a nightmare. The unfolding light of morning revealed the full magnitude of the previous night's terrors. Fallen trees, smoking craters, and large holes marred the forest. Drifter's Folly Memorial Park had fallen silent once more, but it was a haunted silence.

As the day stretched on, the park filled with more people than had occupied its borders in years. They were policemen, detectives, and forensics experts. Eventually, even media representatives showed up, though they were kept at arm's length.

Morning became afternoon. More bodies were found, each drawing expressions of horror from even the most seasoned officers. It took the entire day to recover all the corpses.

But there was one body that wasn't recovered. The authorities spread slowly and deliberately across the park with dogs in tow, searching for a sign of the imposter Fields, the man known as the Hunter. They found only Rodney Crowe, the accomplice who took the Hunter's secrets with him to the grave. The manhunt continued long into the day. Boats were called in to dredge the lake, all to no avail.

Within the forest, a two-way radio roared to life.

"Williams," a voice echoed over the static. "Do you copy?"

The young officer patrolling the forest dutifully answered the call.

"Where are you?" the voice demanded.

"I'm with Stevens," Williams replied.

He kept his eyes open for any sign of life. The forest was abandoned. He couldn't even see any animals.

"Negative," the voice replied. "Stevens just radioed in. He's on his way back."

The wind shifted in his direction, and Williams shivered. He hadn't realized Stevens was gone.

It's too easy to get lost in here, he thought.

"Listen," the voice on the other end of the radio said, "it's getting dark. We're calling off the search for tonight. The last thing we need is an officer out there on his own."

"I understand," Williams replied.

He looked to the sky. Sure enough, the sun had begun to fade. The light dimmed around him. Williams stood on the edge of the lake, his boots covered in the thick mud that cloaked the shore. Dire Lake was beautiful to behold. It was hard to believe it was the scene of such evil.

Beauty or not, the idea of being alone in the woods after dark was far from appealing. He turned to begin the trek uphill. Trees towered around him in every direction.

That was when he spotted it. Something on the forest floor glimmered among the fallen leaves. Williams' brow furrowed. He approached the curious object, inexplicably drawn to it. The policeman knelt down and picked the item up. It fit almost perfectly into his palm.

What is this? Williams thought. He turned the object over in his hands. It looked like a necklace of some kind, though he had never seen anything like it before.

Whispers echoed through the trees, and the wind intensified, scattering leaves around him. Williams glanced up and froze. A set of human footprints led away from the shore, exactly to the spot where he found the strange necklace. His pulse raced as a cold realization settled over him. Someone had emerged from the lake and made their way to shore, leaving the necklace behind.

Something moved at his back. Williams jumped to his feet and pulled his gun from its holster.

"Who's there?" he demanded. The offender, a small bird, flew into the distance. Williams took a few steps back, farther into the forest.

"Williams?" the voice said over the radio.

The police officer ignored it. He followed the path of the footprints with his gaze, searching for where they ended.

When he heard the sound above him, it was already too late. The Hunter came crashing down from the branches where he had hidden, waiting for someone to see the necklace and take the bait. Williams didn't have time to fire in the seconds before the killer landed on him. The two rolled downhill, and Williams lost his grip on the gun. The Hunter was on him in a flash. The killer picked up a rock and bludgeoned the officer's head until he fell still.

The Hunter stared at his kill for a moment, his heart pounding. He was weakened, dehydrated, and covered in burns. His prey had eluded him long ago. He had lost the game.

His gaze fell on the necklace. It called to him as the darkness began to settle in.

The dead policeman's radio sounded again.

"Williams? Do you copy?"

The Hunter snatched the radio from the ground. Fields was dead. He could be Williams for a while yet. Long enough to escape Drifter's Folly and recover. After enough time had passed, he would find Zack Allen and finish what he started.

"Copy that," he said into the radio.

He removed Williams' uniform and dressed himself in the dead man's clothes.

The necklace was right. He hadn't lost. The game had only just begun.

ACKNOWLEDGMENTS

I came up with the idea for this book as I was freezing to death.

I was a senior in high school at the time, and some friends invited me to go camping with them one chilly October evening at Green River Lake. On a dare, I went into the lake after nightfall. The temperature quickly plummeted, and even with layers of clothes and blankets, I was so cold I couldn't sleep. I lay there in the dark for hours, my teeth chattering, unable to rest long after the others had fallen asleep.

There's something vulnerable about sleeping in a tent in the middle of nowhere. As I listened to the noises outside the tent, imagining what might be lurking in the dark, the broad strokes of *A Sound in the Dark* began to form. Well before dawn, the cold finally proved too much for me, and I sought refuge in the warmth of my car. The satisfaction I felt when my teeth stopped chattering on the way home quickly faded when I realized that I had lost my way in the wee hours of the morning.

I received my first laptop for Christmas that year and immediately began working on the story. *A Sound in the Dark* was the first manuscript that I ever attempted to write, but I eventually set it aside without completing it. Many years later, I was finishing my first year of medical school when the rest of the story came to me. So although *A Sound in the Dark* was the first book idea I came up with, it ended up being my eighth completed manuscript!

From the start, *A Sound in the Dark* was always going to be a different animal. Unlike most of my books, it takes place over a single night of terror. I wanted it to be a tight, fast-paced thriller full of twists and turns; as a result, most of the chapters are shorter than usual, with cliffhanger endings intended to keep the reader turning to the next page. At its core, the book is about someone who has lost his sense of purpose finding a reason to keep going. At the time I wrote the book, I was at a crossroads with medical school, unsure whether or not I would make it through, and this theme had a lot of resonance with me. As with many of these stories, writing *A Sound in the Dark* was a way to work out the issues I was facing with school. I also wanted to explore the idea that horrific situations can bring out the best and the worst in people, as we see with Zack and Will, respectively.

There are many people I would like to acknowledge for their help with this book. First off, a huge thank you to my mother—Pam Romines—who was the first to read the manuscript (and then read it over and over again), along with my father—Robert Romines—and my sisters—Allie Romines and Megan White—for their feedback. I would like to acknowledge Michael Garrett, who edited the book. Additionally, I want to thank Betty Ewing and June Anderson for proofreading the story while it was still in the manuscript stage. I also want to thank Streetlight Graphics, the production team that put this book together, including cover design and interior formatting.

And finally, thank *you* for reading! If you enjoyed the story, I encourage you to let me know by leaving a review on Amazon or Goodreads. If you are interested in reading more by me, be sure to check my amazon author page for a list of all my books currently available for purchase. And of course, feel free to contact me if you wish to discuss this story or anything else.

Thanks again,
Kyle

ABOUT THE AUTHOR

Kyle Alexander Romines is a teller of tales from the hills of Kentucky. He enjoys good reads, thunderstorms, and anything edible. His writing interests include fantasy, science fiction, horror, and western.

Kyle's lifelong love of books began with childhood bedtime stories and was fostered by his parents and teachers. He grew up reading *Calvin and Hobbes*, RL Stine's *Goosebumps* series, and *Harry Potter*. His current list of favorites includes Justin Cronin's *The Passage*, *Red Rising* by Pierce Brown, and *Bone* by Jeff Smith. The library is his friend.

His next book, a western, is scheduled to be released in 2017 by Sunbury Press, which has also accepted the sequel to *The Keeper of the Crows* for publication in 2018.

You can contact Kyle at thekylealexander@hotmail.com.

7586

Made in the USA
Lexington, KY
13 September 2017